White Lies
and
Barefaced
Truths

Cathy Hopkins lives in North London with her handsome husband and three deranged cats. Or is it the other way around – her handsome cats and deranged husband? She has had over twenty books published, including the five titles in the Mates, Dates series, and she is currently working on the second book in the Truth, Dare, Kiss or Promise series. Apart from that, she is looking for the answers to why we're here, where we've come from and what it's all about. She is also looking for the perfect hairdresser.

Also available from Piccadilly Press by Cathy Hopkins:

Mates, Dates and Inflatable Bras
Mates, Dates and Cosmic Kisses
Mates, Dates and Portobello Princesses
Mates, Dates and Sleepover Secrets
Mates, Dates and Sole Survivors

Truth, Dare, Kiss or Promise

White Lies
and
Barefaced
Truths

Cathy Hopkins

PICCADILLY PRESS • LONDON

Big thanks to the team at Piccadilly, Rosemary Bromley as always, and Alice Elwes, Lauren Bennie, Scott Brenman, Becca Crewe, Jenni Herzberg, Rachel Hopkins, Annie McGrath and Olivia McDonnell, for answering all my e-mail questions.

First published in Great Britain in 2002
by Piccadilly Press Ltd.,
5 Castle Road, London NW1 8PR

A catalogue record for this book is available from
the British Library

ISBN: 1 85340 751 8 (trade paperback)

3 5 7 9 10 8 6 4

Printed and bound in Great Britain by Bookmarque Ltd.

Design by Judith Robertson
Cover design by Helen Allen, Artpix Design

Set in 11.5/17pt Garamond

Truth, Dare, Kiss or Promise   1

'TRUTH, DARE, kiss or promise?' asked Mac as he attempted to light the fire for the third time.

Becca leaned back against a rock and nuzzled her feet into the sand. 'Truth,' she said.

'OK, you have to tell us who you fancy.'

'Easy,' said Becca. 'Brad Pitt.'

'No, I mean, in the village.'

'Easy again,' said Becca. 'Ollie Axford.'

Mac's face dropped as at last the fire took hold. Although he says he's not into relationships, I reckon he's got a thing for Bec. I saw him staring at her before, when she was combing out her hair. Her hair's her best asset although she doesn't think so. She wants blonde straight hair like Gwyneth Paltrow but she looks more like a Pre-Raphaelite princess with her long Titian coloured mane and perfect alabaster skin.

'Are you honestly telling the absolute truth?' he asked.

I couldn't help but laugh. Typical boy. Just because Becca didn't say she fancied him, he thinks she must be lying.

'Yeah, the absolute real, double honest truth,' said Becca. 'Ollie Axford.'

Mac shrugged his shoulders. 'Don't know what you see in him. He's a right flash git.'

'Exactly,' said Becca. 'That's why I like him. He's different.'

I handed round the Cokes and gave Squidge the sausages to cook. I was thankful I hadn't been asked. I'd have had to say Ollie as well and Squidge wouldn't have liked that, never mind Becca. Squidge has been my boyfriend since junior school but lately, it's all felt flat, I want a bit more excitement. Squidge is so familiar; we grew up together. And it's not that I don't like him. I do, but he's become more of a mate, like family, a brother even. And who wants to snog their brother? *Ewww*. There has to be more. Becca's not the only one who's seen Ollie. Full name Orlando Axford. Son of Zac Axford, famous American rock star who lives out at Barton Hall. Everyone in the village is always on about them, they're *soooo* glamorous. They live in this fab house, more like a mansion, in acres of land with horses and dogs and they've even got a Vietnamese pot-bellied pig. I saw it once by the gate, when I went out there with my dad to deliver their groceries. Mrs Axford is totally gorgeous. She used to be a model and Ollie is the best-looking boy I've ever seen. I haven't ever spoken to him, but I've seen him around when he's been down from school in the holidays.

'OK, your turn, Cat,' said Squidge, putting a sausage on a fork and holding it over the fire. 'Truth, dare, kiss or promise.'

I stared out at the ocean in front of us while I considered which to choose. It was the beginning of September and term started on Monday. Another summer in Cornwall gone and here we all were, the gang, having a beach party before the sun went down. Nothing wrong with any of it, I thought. It is beautiful here and we do have a laugh, it's just, is this is it? Me and Squidge going together until we leave school? No. I want more. And I want it soon.

'Dare,' I said.

Squidge grinned. 'Er, let me think of a good one. Now who we can get you to moon at . . . ?'

Typical. Even the dares are predictable: show your bum to some unsuspecting person.

'No, *no*,' said Becca. 'I have a *much* better dare.'

'You butted in,' I said. 'Show your bum. Butted in. Bum, butt, geddit?'

Mac, Squidge and Becca stared at me as though I was mad. Maybe I am. I have been feeling a bit strange lately. Probably hormones. Mrs Jeffries, our form teacher, puts everything down to that, like when anyone goes off on a wobbly, 'Oh hormones,' she says. We all have a laugh about it, like if anyone acts even slightly weird, we all go, 'It's mi

7

hormones playing me up something rotten.'

'Butthead,' said Becca, 'but I do have a brill dare.'

'Go on then.'

'I dare that the next time you see Ollie Axford, you have to go and talk to him.'

'*Talk* to him. Why?' I asked, fearing for a moment that Becca had sussed my secret.

Becca looked to the heavens. 'For me of course. Oh go on Cat, pleeease, you know how good you are at chatting up boys. And they always like you. Talk to him. Find out if he's noticed me. Find out if he has a girlfriend. That sort of thing, and maybe mention, kind of casually, that you have a friend who'd like to meet him.'

'No way,' I said. 'No, *no* way.'

I looked to Squidge for support.

'Oh go on Cat, if Becca has such a crush, the least you can do as a mate is help her out.'

Astounding. He's not even jealous, threatened. He's so sure of our relationship that he would send me out to chat up the most divine boy in Cornwall, if not the country, and I have his full go ahead.

'No, forget it. I'm not doing dare,' I said. 'I'll choose another one instead.'

'You can't change your mind because you don't like the dare,' objected Becca. 'That's against the rules.'

'Yeah, but what you want me to do is a dare that you should do yourself,' I said looking round at everyone, hoping that one of them would back me up. I could see that Mac had gone into a sulk. Shame, as I really like him. He's been living down here a year now and still hasn't quite landed. He's always going on about London and how he misses his old school and his mates. His mum and dad are divorced, and he lives for the times when he gets to go back to visit his dad who still lives up there in a flat in Islington. Having Becca as a girlfriend might help him settle, and I'm sure she would have been interested if it wasn't for Ollie Axford.

I decided to help him out.

'Truth, dare, kiss or promise, Mac?' I asked.

He shrugged. 'Don't care.'

'Then I'll pick for you,' I said. 'Kiss.'

'I'm not kissing you if that's what you think,' he said, and for a moment his face lightened. 'Squidge would kill me.'

'I never said *who* you have to kiss yet,' I said. 'No, you have to kiss Becca.'

'*Cat!*' said Becca looking shocked. Usually when we played the kiss option, it was to kiss someone geeky at school or one of the ancient locals. One time when we couldn't think of anyone, Becca made Squidge go and kiss a dustbin.

'OK, it has to be at a time when it feels right,' I said backtracking fast.

'That'll be never, then,' said Mac settling back into his sulk. 'And anyway, you haven't really had a proper go, Cat.'

'OK. Truth then,' I said.

'Tell us your biggest secret,' said Becca.

'Wouldn't be a secret then, would it?' I said playing for time.

'Rules are rules and you ducked out of the dare I gave you,' said Becca. 'Come on, spill.'

'OK,' I said, 'but how about I only tell you? There's nothing in the rules that says I have to tell everyone.'

'Fair enough,' said Squidge. 'I know all your secrets anyway.'

Mac shrugged. 'Whatever,' he said turning away and looking out to sea. I think he was pleased that I'd opted out of the dare.

Two packs of sausages, burgers and Cokes later, we set off on the long climb back up the cliff.

'Shouldn't have had that last sausage,' panted Becca after we'd been going ten minutes.

'Almost there,' I said coming up behind her on the path. We stopped for a moment to catch our breath and look at the view stretching out in front of us. Miles and miles of coastline as far as Rame Head. Even though I was born here, I still love watching the sea down below as it breaks on the sand making patterns like white lace.

Squidge and Mac had gone on ahead and had almost reached the top so I decided to tackle Becca while I had her alone.

'Don't you like Mac?' I asked.

Becca pulled her hair up into a ponytail and set off again. 'Yeah, course. But not like that. Besides he's not into having a girlfriend and certainly doesn't fancy me. I could kill you doing that kiss thing on me. Why would you want to set me up with him?'

'I thought you'd like it. I mean, he's your type. Blond, cute smile and he's a laugh most of the time.'

'Ah, but I've set my sights higher,' she said dreamily. 'Ollie Axford. He's The One.'

'That's this week. Last week Phil was The One.'

'Phil Davies? *Ew*. No way,' said Becca. 'Phil was a minor blip in my game plan.'

I had to laugh. No half measures for Becca. She was always in love. Every new boy she had a crush on was 'The One'. I wasn't sure how seriously to take this new infatuation with Ollie. Was it one of her whims or was she for real this time?

As I set off again another thought occurred to me. Why *was* I trying to get her off with Mac? Was it because I wanted the way free, so I could talk to Ollie for me not her?

'Bec.'

'What?'

'I'll tell you my secret now.'

'What?' said Becca stopping again.

'Promise you won't say anything?'

She nodded.

'I think I want to finish with Squidge.' Actually it wasn't my biggest secret. My biggest secret was that I fancied Ollie. But I was careful to omit the word *biggest* and hoped she wouldn't notice.

Becca turned. 'You're kidding. No wonder you didn't want to say in front of the others. But why? I mean you two have been an item since . . . for ever.'

'Exactly. Before the dawn of time, etc.'

'So why now? Has he done something to upset you?'

I laughed. 'Nah.' Squidge would never do anything to upset anyone. He's the nicest person I know. Kind and considerate. Wouldn't harm a fly. Always the first to offer help. Generous. Cool. Cute even. The perfect boyfriend. 'I want a change.'

Becca stared at me. 'Is that why you cut all your hair off?'

'You don't like it do you?'

'I *love* it. It's loads better. You look like Meg Ryan only with dark hair.' We walked on for a bit then Becca turned again. 'Do you fancy someone else? Is that why you want to finish with Squidge?'

I really wanted to tell her, yes, yes I *do*: Ollie. But I couldn't do it. 'Nah,' I said, 'there's nobody else. I just want to move on.'

Becca glanced up at the top of the cliff where the boys were waiting.

'He's going to be devastated. He adores you.'

I followed Becca's glance and Squidge waved down at us. Squidge, lovely lovely Squidge. My pal through thick and thin. He's been there for me in all the good and bad times. Times like when my mum died when I was nine. I've known him that long.

'So when are you going to do it?'

'Don't know,' I said.

'And how? What on earth are you going to say?'

'Double don't know.' I felt awful. I didn't want to hurt him. How was I ever going to find the right words?

Storm in a Teen Cup

'THE TOOTH fairy's not been,' blubbed Emma, as she scrabbled about under her pillow and found the tooth she'd left wrapped in tissue the night before.

I jumped down from the top bunk and went to look for Dad.

'Go away,' snuffled Luke from under his duvet when I poked my head in the boys' room. 'Dad's gone to the market.'

I went to Dad's desk, found a piece of card, scribbled an 'I Owe You' note, then sprinkled it with glitter.

Emma wasn't convinced when I handed it to her.

'The tooth fairy's a bit broke at the moment,' I explained. 'So many children to get round. When she's paid her overdraft off at the Fairy Bank, no doubt she'll be in touch.'

Emma looked like she was going to start crying again, so I found my bag and handed her the Smarties I'd bought yesterday.

'She left you these as well.'

She looked suspiciously at my bag as if to say how come she left them in *your* bag, but she took them, then stuck a couple up her nose. It's her latest game. She sticks sweets up her nose, then snorts them across the room. D'oh thanks, Emma, I thought as I flicked a sticky red one off my arm.

I went downstairs and laid the table for breakfast. That was when Joe (brother number two) decided to experiment with his juice by standing on his head and trying to drink upside down.

Course Emma had to try it as well, but couldn't get up on her head so started doing her whiney act.

At that moment, we heard a loud thump from upstairs. It was Luke, who appeared minutes later rubbing his arm. He'd tried to fly off the top bunk bed. Luckily nothing was broken.

It was then I spied Mogley the cat looking anxiously out of the window of the spin-dryer.

'Eeep!' I squeaked.

'It's her house,' said Emma. 'She likes it.'

As Mogley was frantically scratching to get out, somehow I doubted that. I opened the dryer and pulled her out from amongst the damp laundry and she purred happily in my arms. I was thankful that I'd got to her before anyone had switched it on.

There was peace for about ten minutes as we tucked into rounds of toast and honey, then I sent them off to get dressed. Or so I thought. It wasn't long before Joe came mumbling into the kitchen. He'd glued his back teeth together. He was sticking something down for his science project and put the glue tube in his mouth while he used his hands.

I gave him a glass of milk to swill round his mouth and, thank God, his teeth unlocked, but when Dad came back, the house was pandemonium. Emma wanted to do the glue trick to try and pull more of her teeth out, the laundry was all over the table where I'd been trying to remove the cat hairs, there was juice all over the floor from Joe's upside down drinking experiment and, next door, Luke had the telly on full blast.

'I can't leave you alone for five minutes,' said Dad taking in the scene before him. 'And look at you Cat, you're not even out of your pyjamas yet and it's already nine o'clock.'

'But . . .' I started.

'No buts about it,' said Dad. 'It's about time all of you learnt to behave properly.'

Sometimes I give up. But then, it's nothing new. It's only another typical Saturday morning in the Kennedy household.

'Cat, I need you to go into Kingsand and pick up a few things,' said Dad giving me a list later that morning.

'But Dad, I was going to go over to Becca's,' I began.

'You can go this afternoon, morning's for jobs.'

I couldn't argue as the others were all busy with their chores. Chores that no doubt I'd have to do again for them when I got back. Joe and Luke's idea of tidying their bedroom is to hide everything under their duvets. I'm forever clearing out old sweet wrappers, video games and assorted bits of clothing when they fall into bed at night.

I set off to the village and bought the items Dad wanted from the shop. There weren't many people about, only the occasional tourist strolling through the lanes admiring the coloured sandstone cottages and pots of flowers displayed everywhere. Kingsand prides itself on its appearance and has won the 'Best Kept Village' award many times.

I made my way down the narrow pavement towards the bay at the bottom. I wouldn't like to live here, I thought, as I gazed into some of houses lining the lane. It must be like this all the time — having strangers pass by and stare into your living room. In one window, a family sat around the table as their mum gave them breakfast. I turned away. Sometimes it still hurts seeing cosy families with a mum. I wonder if they know how lucky they are.

I decided to walk through the village to the next bay at Cawsand. Kingsand and Cawsand are twin villages, right next to each other, both with sandy bays that are easy to get to. Before she was ill, Mum used to bring us to Cawsand Bay as it's safe for swimming. We'd sit for hours watching the boats and people playing on the beach.

I made my way through the village, then down into the square at Cawsand, then turned into the bay. There were only a couple of people: a woman having a coffee at the café and a boy at the far end of the beach.

I went and sat by the rocks on the left and stared out at the sea. Some days I really miss mum. Most of the time I'm OK. I'm fourteen and I know she's gone and not coming back. But some days I don't feel so grown up and I wish she was here and I could cuddle up and feel looked after. Being grown-up can be confusing sometimes and I don't know what I want. I'm sure she'd have understood. Must be mi old hormones playing me up, I thought, as I brushed away a tear.

Suddenly the boy from the other end of the beach plonked himself down next to me on the sand. I'd been so caught up in my thoughts that I hadn't heard him approaching.

'It is lovely here isn't it?' he said, indicating the bay with a sweep of his hand.

I looked round at him and my chest tightened.

Ohmigo-o-o-od. It was Ollie Axford. Ollie Axford sitting right next to me in a black T-shirt and shorts. He stretched long tanned legs out in front of him. Totally, totally gorgeous. Jet black hair, denim blue eyes and a cute dimple on his chin.

'Cat got your tongue.' He was smiling.

I realised I must have been staring at him. Ogling, more like.

'Actually that's my name.'

He looked puzzled.

'Cat. Short for Catherine, but everyone calls me Cat.'

'Nice,' he said looking me up and down in a way that made me blush. 'That's a nice name. Suits you. You look like a cat sitting here on your own. You don't scratch do you?'

I laughed. 'Only if provoked. Then I bite as well.'

He grinned and raised an eyebrow. 'Oh really. Sounds dangerous. So I'd better be nice. Will you purr if I stroke you?'

And he began to gently stroke my arm. Ohmigod, ohmigod, *ohmigod*.

'We have cats up at the house,' he continued. 'They're very independent, aren't they? Are you like that?'

'Suppose I can be.'

He leaned close. 'But they can be very affectionate as well if they like you.'

I laughed. 'Yeah, but you have to be deserving.'

I couldn't believe it. I was flirting with him and he was flirting back. Ollie Axford. And me. On the beach. On our own. *Arghhhh.*

'Then I'd better be extra nice, hadn't I? Because I like cats,' he said. 'I'm Ollie by the way. Ollie Axford.'

'I know.'

He turned his head and looked at me quizzically causing my chest to tighten even more. I could hardly breath.

'How?'

'Oh, everyone knows who you are. You live at Barton Hall, don't you?'

He nodded. 'Yeah. How do you know that?'

'My dad owns the shop over in the next village. Um, your mum comes in sometimes.'

He seemed to be happy with that. 'So Cat. What do you do around here?'

'Do like what? What do you mean?'

He settled himself back against my rock so that his arm was touching mine. 'Tell me everything. Who you are. What you're doing here all on your own.'

'Er . . .' What could I say to make it interesting? He seemed to be enjoying my discomfort.

'OK, start with where you go to school.'

'Near Torpoint. Everyone round here goes there pretty well.'

'Oh yeah, Torpoint. My sister's going to go there.'

'Your sister?'

'Yeah, she starts on Monday. She was at school in London but hated it. She wanted to be closer to home, so Mum and Dad got her changed.'

Now this *was* interesting. I'd heard that he had a sister but I'd never seen her. Maybe he was going to change schools as well. That would cause a stir. Ollie Axford at our school. I couldn't wait to tell Becca. She'd think she'd died and gone to heaven. Ohmigod. Becca. I remembered the dare that I'd turned down, but now I had the perfect opportunity. I had to mention her or she'd kill me when I told her that I'd bumped into Ollie. I sat up so that we weren't touching any more.

'And, er, are you going to change schools as well?'

'No way,' he said. 'I like my school. But look out for Lia, will you? That's my sister. She's a good kid and you know, starting a new school can be a bit daunting sometimes.'

He seemed nice. I liked that he was watching out for his sister.

'I'll make a point of it,' I said. 'How old is she?'

'Fourteen, so she'll be going into Year Nine.'

'That's my year. So yeah, I'll watch out for her.'

Ollie leaned up so that he was touching me again. 'But what about you? You haven't told me much yet.'

I shrugged. 'Not a lot to tell. I grew up here. I've got two stupid brothers and a sister who I think may be an alien.'

'Older or younger?'

'Younger. Luke's ten, Joe's eight and Emma's the baby, she's just turned six. You?'

'Two sisters. One older, Star – she's up in London. And Lia.'

'Two? Bet they spoil you being an only boy.'

'I wish. And are you married, single or divorced?'

'Divorced,' I said. 'He got the kids, I kept the houses.'

He laughed. 'Seriously, though.'

'Um . . . there's a gang of us that hang out, you know.

Like mates . . . you know . . .' Why wasn't I telling him the truth? That I had a steady boyfriend.

'So what are you doing sitting down here all on your own?'

I looked down at the sand. 'Oh, nothing.'

'Looked like you had something on your mind to me. Come on, spill. I'm a good listener.'

'I was . . . I was thinking about my mum.'

'Why? Had a barney?'

'No. She used to bring me here when I was little. She died five years ago. I . . . I miss her and this place kind of brings her back.' I didn't know why I was telling him this. I hadn't told anyone this was my special place when I want to feel close to her. I learned pretty quickly after she died that some people feel uncomfortable when they hear about death. Like they don't know what to say, or they come out with something stupid and it's obvious that they're embarrassed and feel sorry for me, and I hate that.

But Ollie was looking at me kindly. I made myself smile. 'Sorry. I'm not usually like this. I was just thinking of her today and felt a bit sad.'

'Understandable,' he said. 'It means you loved her a lot.' He leapt to his feet. 'Come on, let me buy you an ice cream and we'll go for a paddle.'

I looked down at the shopping at my feet, then up at the vision standing only a foot away, grinning at me. Sorry Dad, I thought. You'll have to wait. Opportunities like this don't come along every day, not down here they don't.

And I still had to mention Becca.

We spent the next hour gabbing about everything. He was really nice. No, not nice, gorgeous, gorgeous, *gorgeous* and he made me feel the same. Like I was the most interesting, scintillating person on the planet.

'Eep!' I said looking at my watch. 'Got to go.'

'Eep?' he laughed. 'What kind of word is that?'

I laughed back. 'It's the noise our computer at home makes if I make a mistake on it. Eep. Eep. It's kind of got into my brain and now if I ever do something wrong, out it comes as a warning.'

He took my hand. 'And are you doing something wrong now?'

Eep, eep, eep, went a voice in my head as a delicious, warm sensation flooded through me. 'Er, no, just . . . should have been back ages ago.' I'd been on the beach with him for a long time. I still hadn't mentioned Becca and he was holding my hand. Eep, double eep.

'Er, um, Ollie?'

'Yes,' he said linking his fingers through mine.

'Um, er, I've got a friend, that is, have you ever noticed anyone about the village?'

Ollie began playing with my fingers and I felt like my brain was going to fuse.

'I've noticed lots of people round the village. The lady in the Post Office, the –'

'No, I mean, any girls.'

Ollie grinned. 'I notice all the girls.'

'But, see this one in particular.' It wasn't coming out right. I made myself think straight. 'See, I have this friend.'

'Ah,' said Ollie looking right into my eyes. 'A friend. OK. So what about this *friend*?'

'Well, she's noticed you and . . .' I didn't know that someone just looking at you could cause such chaos inside. It felt like time had slowed down yet my heart had sped up. I could hear it thumping in my chest.

Ollie put his other hand up to my neck and ran his fingers softly through my hair. 'Oh, has she now? So tell me more about this . . . friend.'

Eep, eep, eeeeep. 'Well, I think she kind of likes you and . . .'

He pulled me towards him and kissed me. A lovely soft kiss that went right down to the tips of my toes and back.

'I've been wanting to do that since I first saw you,' he whispered nuzzling into my neck.

EEEEEEP. I pulled back.

'What's the matter?' he asked.

'Nothing. Just got to go. Um, thanks for the ice cream. And . . .'

I began to walk backwards away from him. 'Bye, thanks, sorry.'

He stood there grinning. 'Any time, Cat. Hope to see you and your *friend* around.'

I ran all the way home feeling exhilarated. Just before I reached our house, I stopped to catch my breath. Ollie Axford had kissed me and I was floating on air. But he was Becca's. She'd bagged him first. And I already had a boyfriend. I should have told Becca the truth, my biggest secret, while I had the chance. What was I going to do? What was I going to say to Becca? She'd kill me. Never speak to me again.

I set off again more slowly. Got to think this through. Becca's been my friend for years. My best friend and she's more important than any boy. And I'd tried to do her dare for her even when I'd been let off the hook. It wasn't my fault that Ollie misunderstood about my 'friend'. Got to think this through.

As I put the key in the lock and braced myself for the telling off for being late, there was one thing that I knew for certain. That fabulous sensation was how I wanted to feel when I was kissed. I had to tell Squidge it was over. There were other boys besides Ollie. So maybe I couldn't have him, but there were others. There could be others. I'd blank Ollie out. Put him in a box in my head and lock the door. History. Pretend it never happened.

But as Dad went into his inquisition, all I could think about was how it felt when Ollie's lips touched mine. And how I felt when he held my hand. I couldn't stop it. He'd escaped from the box and a part of my brain had gone into action replay, action replay, action replay. And with each time, the feeling when he kissed me came back.

Oh, eep.

Fifty Ways to Leave Your Lover

Dear Squidge,

I really like you but . . .

I RIPPED up the paper. Pathetic.

'Oh, how am I going to do this, Bec? *Help* me.'

'Only if you tell me again about Ollie,' said Becca staring dreamily out of her bedroom window.

'I've *told* you six times already,' I said getting up from her desk and going to lie on her bed.

'I know, but I love hearing. Tell me how he looked again.'

Divine, I thought. Sexy. Gorgeous. Stunning.

'He looked all right, I suppose.'

'All right? You must be blind. But you did really mention me, didn't you? You're not making it up?'

'No I *really* mentioned you. First I asked if he'd noticed

anyone around the village and he said loads of people . . .'

'Then you said about me?'

'Yeah I told you already. He said he noticed all the girls.'

'So maybe he has noticed me?'

'Maybe he has.'

'Did you describe me or anything? Say anything nice about me?'

'I did try, Bec, honestly, but it wasn't easy. I had a load of shopping with me and I had to get back with it and . . .'

'I know,' said Becca, 'and I am grateful. Going up and just talking to him out of the blue. I could never have done that. You're such a pal.

I am a cow. A cow, cow, cow, I thought. I'd told her what I could. Not about the kiss of course. Or the holding hands. Or the flirting. I'd just told her the bits in between.

'And Lia's starting school on Monday?' she asked.

'Yes. He said she was. I told you.'

'And you have to watch out for her. And I will too. And hopefully get to meet him.'

'Yeah. Now *please*, help me come up with a way to finish with Squidge.'

'You could text him.'

I shook my head. 'Couldn't. Too cold. Like what would I say?'

'U R dumped.'

I threw a pillow at her. 'Heartless.'

'OK by fax.'

'Oh, very funny. Not.'

'By phone, then you have some security in case he wants to kill you.'

'And I wouldn't have to see his face. Oh Bec, this is awful, I really, really, really don't want to hurt him.'

'Then stay with him.'

I went back to my letter. 'Maybe this is best as he'll have time to read it in private and get used to the idea.'

'Isn't there a song about ways to leave your lover?'

'Yeah. "Fifty Ways to Leave Your Lover" by Paul Simon. Dad's got it on a CD in the car. But try naming one.'

Becca looked thoughtful. 'You could move abroad.'

'Get real.'

'You could get him to finish with you.'

'How?'

'Behave horribly. Like always be late and in a bad mood. Pick your nose and eat it.'

'Urrghhh Becca. *Gross*. Besides if I did act horrid, knowing Squidge and what a sweetie he is, he'd be all understanding and try and make me feel better.'

'Join the Foreign Legion.'

'Thanks, you're being really helpful.'

'Tell him you've had the God call and are going to be a nun.'

'Yeah, like he'd believe that.'

'Say you've gone lesbo.'

'Then you'd have to pretend to be my girlfriend.'

'*Ewww*. Get lost. No listen, if you want my real and honest opinion I think you should just go round and tell him face-to-face. You owe him that much seeing as you've been together so long. And it shouldn't be so difficult as you know each other so well.'

She was right. I did owe him that much. I'd bite the bullet, take the bull by its horns, all that sort of thing. I could do it.

So why was I feeling so terrified?

'Jack,' Mrs Squires called up the stairs, 'Cat's here. Come in, love.'

I followed her through into their kitchen. I usually feel so comfortable here, it's like my second home. The Squires family have lived in Cawsand for generations in the same little cottage in one of the lanes at the back of the village. Their ancestors were fishermen, but now his mum and dad are The Most Important People In the Village, as his dad runs the local garage and his mum is a hairdresser. Mr Squires fixes my dad's old van, which is forever breaking down, and Mrs Squires cuts my hair and colours Squidge's. This month his is dyed white blond like Spike's in 'Buffy the Vampire Slayer'. Squidge has even got a three-quarter length leather coat to complete the look. Mr and Mrs Squires are really nice. Normal. I like going there and hope I still can when I finish with Squidge. I hope we can still be mates.

'You're looking a bit peaky, Cat. Are you all right?' asked Mrs Squires.

'Yeah, fine,' I said going over to play with Amy, who was sitting in her high chair. 'Can I pick her up?'

'Course you can,' said Mrs Squires going back into the hall. 'JACK, Cat's here.'

It always sounds strange to hear him called Jack as everyone calls him Squidge except his mum and dad. He doesn't look like a Jack. He looks like a Squidge. We call him that partly because of his surname, Squires, but mainly because ever since he was tiny, he's been obsessed with cameras. He was always looking at the world through a lens and forever squidging up his eyes to focus. Still is.

'Come up,' called Squidge from upstairs.

'Next time,' I said to Amy and she acknowledged my presence by putting her bowl of mashed banana on her head and gurgling happily.

I took a deep breath and headed up the stairs. I still wasn't sure what I was going to say, but I was determined somehow or other to find the words.

Squidge was lying on his bed. 'Hey,' he said.

'Hey. What are you doing?'

'Nothing.'

This wasn't like Squidge. He was always doing something. Full of ideas or working on something.

'What's up?' I asked.

He showed me a letter and a brochure. 'This. It's that

course I wanted to do in London in half-term, you know, about story structure.'

I took the brochure from him. He'd been talking about this course for ages. Apparently all the film people do it and as Squidge's thing is to write and direct his own films, he'd been looking forward to it eagerly. He's been getting up at the crack of dawn to do a newspaper round over the summer to save up.

'Costs three hundred and something pounds. No way can I afford that.'

'Have you asked your parents?'

Squidge shook his head. 'Nah, with Amy, Mum can't work as much as she used to. And Tom's starting secondary school, so . . . you know . . .'

I sat on the end of his bed and squeezed his foot. 'Sorry.'

'I thought it would be about forty quid or something. I've saved a hundred for my train and stuff, and Mac said I could stay at his dad's, but no way can I afford the course.' He sighed. 'Just as you think everything's working out, something like this comes along and ruins it all.'

He looked so sad. This isn't the time, I thought. I couldn't finish with him today. It would be the last straw.

'Want to play aeroplanes?' I asked.

Squidge forced a smile. 'Sure.'

I climbed on to the end of the bed and he raised his legs into the air while I balanced my abdomen on his feet.

'Ready,' he said.

'Ready,' I said.

Squidge raised his feet with me on them, held on to my shoulders and I flung my arms wide as his feet flew me through the air. That's aeroplanes. At least it got him to laugh.

Mr Squires popped his head in the door and found me in mid-flight.

'Honestly you two, you never grow up, do you?'

Sex Education

'HOW MANY times do you have to have sex to have a baby, Cat?' asked Joe as we finished wiping the supper dishes.

'Only once as far as I know,' I said.

Joe looked thoughtful. 'So that means Mum and Dad had sex four times.'

'How do you work that out?'

Joe counted on his fingers. 'You, me, Luke and Emma. Four of us.'

'I guess,' I said trying not to laugh. 'But maybe you'd better ask Dad about that sort of thing.'

Joe went into the living room where Dad was watching the news and Emma got up from the table to follow him.

'Private conversation,' I said. 'Leave them alone.'

She went and lay on the floor in the hall and was clearly doing her best to listen in.

'He's telling about how babies are made,' she whispered back to me.

A short while later, the door opened and Joe came out shaking his head. 'Yuck,' he said. 'Disgusting. You don't want to know.'

Dad followed him out and saw Luke doing his home-work at the kitchen table.

'I've just been talking to Joe about the facts of life, Luke. Is there anything you'd like to know?'

Luke went scarlet and buried his head in his geography book. 'Go away Dad,' he muttered into the book.

Dad shrugged, went back to watch the news and that was the end of that. Or so I thought.

I was in the local Spar on Sunday morning with Emma doing some shopping when it happened. I'd just put some eggs in the trolley when Emma piped up.

'Better not let Dad or the boys near those or we'll have babies and there's not enough room for them at our house.'

'What do you mean?' I asked.

'I heard him telling Joe the other night. You need an egg and a willie and then you get a baby.'

I laughed. 'Not these kind of eggs, Emma. The eggs that make babies are already inside of you.'

Emma looked at her tummy. 'Where?'

'Um, in your ovaries. They're tiny and there's loads and loads of them. Oh, you'll understand later. Ask Dad when you're older.'

'But I am old,' she said. 'Six. That's *really* old.'

I quickly wheeled the trolley to the checkout and my stomach did a double flip. There was Ollie Axford with one of his mates.

He turned and smiled when he saw me. 'Cat,' he said.

Before I could say anything, Emma had caught me up and tugged on his hand. 'How many willies have you got?'

Ollie looked faintly surprised while his mate giggled behind him. 'Er, only one last time I looked.'

'My dad's got *four* willies,' said Emma in a loud voice.

I wanted to die.

'This is Emma,' I said, 'the alien I told you about. Why on earth do you think Dad has got four willies, Em?'

'You need a willie and an egg, I told you. There's four of us in our family so dad must have four willies.'

By now, half the shop was listening in and Ollie's mate was holding his sides laughing.

'Aw . . . cute.' Ollie was smiling.

The checkout next to us opened up and I quickly wheeled my trolley there, paid my money and ran.

When I got home, Luke called me into the boys' room where we kept our family computer.

'There was an e-mail from Squidge for you,' he said. 'He's coming over.'

Good, I thought. No time like the present and this time I'll be ready. Seeing Ollie again had double convinced me that it was time to finish with Squidge. Not because I was after Ollie, but he'd reminded me what it could feel like to really fancy someone. I wished I could talk to Becca about it all truthfully, but I knew that was a no-no. This was the first time in all our years of friendship that I hadn't told her the whole story. But at least I could come clean with Squidge. It was a new term tomorrow and I wanted to start with a fresh slate and all that. A new beginning all round.

This time I'd planned exactly what I was going to say, complete with the obligatory 'can we still be friends?' at the end. And I'd mean it.

Squidge arrived as I was putting away the groceries. He had a big grin on his face, so he'd clearly got over his disappointment of yesterday. Fantastic, I thought. Squidge never stays down for long.

I took a deep breath and plunged in, 'I'm really glad you came, because I have something I want to talk to you about.'

'OK, he said, 'but me first. I've also got something I want to say.'

'OK.'

He rummaged around in his rucksack and pulled out a small package wrapped in purple shiny paper. 'I went over to Plymouth yesterday after you'd been over and I got you a wee prezzie,' he said handing it to me.

'Oh, Squidge, you shouldn't have,' I said. Oh, Squidge you *really* shouldn't have, I thought.

'Go on, open it.'

I ripped off the paper and opened the box inside. It was a jeweller's box and inside was the most perfect silver bracelet.

Squidge's grin stretched from ear to ear. 'The shop girl told me it's from a place in New York called Tiffany. See, I wanted to get you something really special to say I think you're the best friend anyone could ever have. Not just yesterday, but all the time we've known each other. Look on the inside, see it's engraved.'

I turned the bracelet over and there in tiny letters was, 'To Cat with love'.

'Squidge, this must have cost a fortune.'

Squidge shrugged. 'You deserve it. See, I know how hard it is for you sometimes, and yesterday kind of made me realise I'd been a bit selfish lately, obsessed with doing my film course and saving money and here's you having to be like a mum to Joe and Emma and Luke. You haven't had anything new for ages and I thought, what a pig I am, I've neglected you. So this is to say I do appreciate you.'

'You . . . you haven't spent your course money on this, have you?'

'Might have done,' he smiled. 'But you're worth it, Cat. So what's a stupid film course?'

'But Squidge, all those paper rounds . . .'

Squidge took my hand and looked into my eyes. 'What's important is having a mate like you. You've always been there for me when I needed you, making me

laugh, listening to all my mad ideas. I wanted to do something nice for you. Now come on, put it on.'

He fastened the bracelet on my wrist. 'Looks fab,' he
said turning my wrist over to admire it then gently kissing
the palm of my hand. 'Now. Your turn. What was it you
wanted to say?'

I looked at the bracelet and Squidge's smiling open face.

'Oh nothing important. Stuff like, you ready for school
tomorrow?'

Back to School

'SUNITA AHMED,' read Mrs Jeffries.

'Here, Miss.'

'David Alexander.'

'Here.'

'Mary Andrews.'

'Present.'

'Ophelia Moonbeam Axford.'

A titter went round the class.

'Here, Miss,' said a stunning-looking girl a couple of desks away. 'But please, everyone calls me Lia.'

As Mrs Jeffries continued calling the register, everyone turned round to look at the new girl. All through assembly everyone had been wondering who she was. Course Bec and I had guessed. It was Ollie's sister. She looked so like him, the same denim blue eyes in a perfect heart-shaped face, the only difference was that her long hair was white blond whereas Ollie's was dark.

Mrs Jeffries had reached the Ks.

'Mark Keegan?'

'Yes, Miss.'

'Catherine Kennedy.'

'Here, Miss, but everyone calls me Cat.'

I smiled cheekily over at Lia and she smiled back. Not Mrs Jeffries, though.

'Anyone *else* want to be known by a name besides the one they were born with?'

Half the class put up their hands.

'Yes. And you can call me Madam,' she said wearily. 'Now where was I? Ah yes. *Catherine* Kennedy.'

'Here, Miss,' I said. Best not start the new term on the wrong foot.

At break I saw that Lia was hanging back as the rest of the class charged for the door. Ollie had been right. It was hard starting a new school, especially in Year Nine when everyone already knew each other. I felt for her, as she looked a bit lost and lonely.

'Do you know where to go?' I asked.

'Not really,' she said.

'Come with me and I'll show you round. This is Becca,' I said as Becca ambled over to join us.

As we gave her the grand tour of the essentials – the loos, the library and the best places to hang out without being hassled by teachers, I noticed that Becca had gone quiet. Unusual for her, as most days she never shuts up.

In the playground I spotted Squidge and Mac in a corner by the bike sheds, so I took Lia over to meet them. And *they* were quiet and shy. What was going on?

'What year are you in?' asked Lia.

'Year Eleven,' chorused Squidge and Mac, then stood there all gawky and gangly. Then it dawned on me: they were intimidated.

Lia was beautiful and somehow her presence had turned them stupid.

'Let's go and sit over there,' I said pointing at an empty bench. 'See you later, boys.'

Becca stayed behind with them for a moment and, as Lia and I sat down, I could tell they were talking about her.

'Do you always have that effect on boys?' I asked.

'What do you mean?' said Lia.

'They're gobsmacked.'

Lia looked over at them. 'Why?'

'Gorgeous girl turns them into jelloid,' I laughed.

'Who me? You're kidding.'

Becca came over to join us and sat awkwardly on the end of the bench. This is silly, I thought. I have to break the ice.

'Ophelia Moonbeam. Is that really your name?'

'I know. It's awful isn't it? I *hate* it.'

'But it's so romantic,' said Becca finding her tongue at last. 'Like Ophelia in Hamlet and in all those Pre-Raphaelite paintings.'

Lia nodded, 'Yeah, we did them in art at my old school.

But have you seen that painting of Ophelia by John Millais? All tragic-looking and drowning in the river. Apparently she had to get into a bath to be painted and got pneumonia after. Not so romantic.'

Becca looked miffed. 'I think it's a beautiful painting. I've got a poster of it on my wall. People say *I* look like a Pre-Raphaelite.'

Eep, I thought. Better step in, but Lia got there first.

'You do,' she said 'but you're more of a Burne-Jones princess than a trago-queen.'

Becca tossed her hair and seemed appeased.

'So why Moonbeam?' I asked.

'Mad parents. They're stuck in another era and have given us all weird names,' replied Lia. 'Like my older sister, she's called Star, my brother's called Orlando, then me, Ophelia Moonbeam. How naff it that?'

Becca perked up. 'Orlando. That's a nice name.'

I caught Becca's eye. I'd wondered how long it was going to be before she brought *him* up.

'We call him Ollie,' said Lia.

'Oh really,' said Becca going into her wide eyed and innocent act. 'And how old is your brother? . . . Oh, *and* your sister?'

'Star's twenty. She lives up in London. She's a model. And Ollie's seventeen. He goes to school in London. I used to go as well but I didn't like it. I like being at home, so Mum got me a place here.'

Becca wasn't to be distracted. 'But don't you miss Ollie when he's away? Oh, and Star, of course.'

I had to laugh to myself. She was being so obvious, but Lia hadn't cottoned on. She had no reason to know that we already knew who Ollie was.

'Yes I miss them, but Ollie comes down a lot at the weekends. At least once a month. And Star whenever she can.'

There was no stopping Becca now. 'What's he like?'

'He's OK. You know, usual brother stuff.'

'Does he look like you?' asked Becca, who had happily settled herself on the bench by now.

'Sort of, only he's got dark hair. Anyway, why are you so interested in him?'

Becca sighed and indicated the groups of boys in the playground. 'Take a look around. This is it. The local talent. Not up to much.'

'Mac and Squidge look nice,' said Lia.

'Oh Squidge is Cat's boyfriend. Or was. Or is. Have you done it yet?'

'Done what, Cat?' asked Lia.

I really didn't want to get into all this. I'd only just met Lia and already I was to be known as Cat and Squidge. Exactly what I didn't want.

'Ended it. We've been together for years and er, well, I think it's time to finish with him.'

'Look what he bought her,' said Becca pointing at my bracelet.

'It's beautiful,' said Lia. 'So why do you want to finish with him exactly? He looks kind of cute to me.'

'Yes, why *do* you want to finish with him exactly?' echoed Becca. 'I can't say I really understand. He's *sooo* nice. I mean, you get on, he buys you lovely presents, he's good looking, good company . . .'

I wanted to kill her. It was hard enough as it was. Even a voice in my own head kept asking, are you doing the right thing? Maybe I was about to make the biggest mistake of my whole life and I'd never meet anyone as lovely again. Never have another boyfriend. Ever. Both Lia and Becca were looking at me waiting for me to answer.

I remembered a line from telly the night before. 'The magic's gone,' I said.

Lia nodded. 'I had a boyfriend up in London like that. He was perfect in every way, but it was like there was no excitement left. I got bored.'

'So what did you do?'

Lia blushed. 'I'm afraid I took the cowardly way out and got my friend to tell him.'

I looked hopefully at Becca. 'No way, Cat. Don't look at me. You're on your own here. So Lia, when's Ollie down again?'

'A few weeks,' said Lia. 'He only went back last night. Why, do you want to meet him?'

Becca's face lit up. 'Yeah, maybe.'

'Then I have to warn you,' said Lia, 'Ollie may be my

brother, but he's a legendary heartbreaker.'

'In what way?' asked Becca, who had given up all attempts at being cool and was literally hanging on to Lia's every word.

'There's a trail of girls after him up in London, always phoning him. His longest relationship lasted about three weeks. His idea of commitment is to ask for someone's e-mail address. He strings girls along, makes them fall in love with him, then drops them.'

'Maybe he's not met the right one,' said Becca dreamily.

'That's what they all hope,' said Lia as Becca's face fell. 'He's even started down here. The other day, he said he'd snogged some girl on the beach. Poor girl I say, another one bites the dust.'

Eep. My heart began to thump in my chest. Did she know it was me? He had asked me to look out for her and maybe he'd told her. Then Becca would *know* it was me.

'Who?' demanded Becca.

Lia shrugged. 'Don't know. Some local girl, I guess. He said he liked her, though, and that they had a really long talk.'

Ohmigod. Ohmigod.

Becca was looking daggers at me.

'Er, excuse us for a mo Lia, I have to talk to Cat about something.'

Lia looked puzzled as Becca got up and beckoned me to follow her. 'Er, come on Cat. You know that, er, project we were working on. We need to go over a few things.'

I got up to follow her. Eep. Eep. I wished I'd told her the truth in the beginning.

Once inside the school, Becca hauled me into the science lab and turned on me. 'So you were there. Did you see him with anyone?'

I sighed with relief. She hadn't automatically thought it was me. 'Er no. But I was only there a short while, I told you.'

Becca's eyes were drilling into me. Tell the truth, I thought. Tell the truth.

'So was there anyone else around?' she asked. 'Anyone he could have got talking to after you left.'

'No. Only an older lady having a coffee.' I felt as if I was being interrogated by police on 'The Bill' or something. Honest, guv, it weren't me.

Becca looked thoughtful. 'It could have been anyone. Probably that tart, Megan Wilson, from Year Ten. She's always hanging about in Cawsand.'

'Yeah. Maybe. It could have been anyone.'

Oh argh. Double argh.

White Lies

WHEN I got home the following Friday, there was a delicious aroma of garlic and onions wafting from the kitchen. Oh fab, I thought, Jen's here.

I followed the smell and found her busy chopping peppers. It looked like she'd just come from work as she still had her air hostess uniform on underneath Dad's Homer Simpson apron. She works over in Plymouth and does the local flights up to Bristol or London and back.

'Hungry?' she asked, smoothing a stray tendril of hair back into place. She always looked so smart. Slim and blond with her hair twisted back into a neat French plait.

'Always am when you're here.' I smiled.

I liked Jen. Dad's been seeing her for over a year now and when she comes over, she likes to cook for us. It's a real treat, as Dad's not quite mastered the art of cooking. His idea of culinary delight is to put cheese in with the mash, which is usually served with burgers or sausages. And my specialities are pasta, pasta or pasta – anything that's quick and easy, so Jen's cooking is a welcome change.

'I'm doing a chicken casserole, that OK?'

I nodded. 'Need a hand?'

'You could chop those leeks for me,' she said pointing to the vegetable basket.

As we busied ourselves in the kitchen, Jen proceeded to do the usual adult interrogation. 'So how's school?'

'OK,' I said.

'You've gone into Year Nine, haven't you?'

I nodded and started setting the table.

'You seem subdued tonight,' she said. 'Not like you.'

I shrugged, then I guess I must have sighed, because she picked up on it in a second.

'School trouble?'

'No, school is fine. In fact it's nice to be back in a strange way. There's a new girl started called Lia. She's been hanging out with me and Bec all week. I think we're going to be friends. She's Zac Axford's daughter.'

'Oh, from Barton Hall?'

I nodded then rummaged in the cupboard for glasses.

'So what's up, then?' persisted Jen. 'Boy trouble? Friend trouble?'

I hesitated. I really needed to talk to someone about all the strange goings on in my head lately and Becca was off limits at the moment, and Dad, well Dad was never the easiest person to have a real conversation with.

'Both,' I said. 'Promise you won't tell anyone, not Dad or anyone.'

'Promise.'

'I've been thinking a lot lately about truth.'

Jen laughed. 'Oh, philosophical trouble.'

I smiled. 'Sort of. See, sometimes you don't tell the truth to protect someone, right?'

Jen nodded. 'Right.'

'Sometimes to just keep the peace and sometimes not to hurt someone. But it's not easy. Like what would you do if you knew if you told someone the truth it would upset them. But truth and lies, both can hurt can't they?'

Jen looked at me with concern. 'I guess. But it sounds serious. You going to tell me what this is really about?'

I hesitated again then decided I could trust Jen. She was OK for a grown-up. 'Well, it's about Squidge mainly. You know we've been going together for ages now?'

Jen nodded.

'Well, I've been trying to finish with him and it's really difficult. It never seems to be the right time and I don't want to hurt him. That's where telling the truth is hard, you know what I mean?'

Jen nodded again. 'It's always difficult finishing with someone.'

'So what do I do?'

Jen stopped her preparations. 'In a situation like this, honesty is always the best policy. Trying to protect someone from the truth can prolong the agony.'

'Tell me about it,' I interrupted.

'But for him as well as for you. If the situation was the other way round, say he wanted to finish with you, you'd want to know, wouldn't you?'

'Yeah. Definitely.'

'You've got to be cruel to be kind sometimes. It's only respectful if you care about someone, and you clearly do about Squidge. Be straight with him. Take a deep breath and tell him where you're at. Otherwise you're giving him false hope that everything's all right when it's not. He needs to be able to move on as well as you.'

She was right. I owed Squidge the truth, it wasn't fair otherwise.

Jen was looking at me kindly. 'It will be all right, Cat. Life goes on.'

I nodded. 'I know. You're right. I'll tell him.'

At that moment Emma burst in, 'Tarzan in the jungle, had a bellyache, couldn't find a toilet. Thwup, too late.'

Jen and I burst out laughing. 'Lovely,' said Jen. 'And where did you learn that? School?'

'No,' said Emma. 'Joe.'

At supper, Emma and Joe insisted that Jen serve dinner like an air hostess. Poor Jen. I felt sorry for her. On her few days off, she comes here and they make her do her work routine.

'After dinner,' she said into the soup ladle that she was using as a pretend microphone, 'I'll be coming down the corridor by the fridge serving dessert. On tonight's menu, we have a choice of chocolate chip ice cream or . . . or nothing. After that we'll be showing a video in the living room and turning the lights out so that passengers who wish to, can sleep.'

Dad laughed and looked at her appreciatively. It was good to see him happy and he always was when she was around.

After supper I went upstairs to start my weekend homework. It's a difficult task seeing as we only have one proper table in the house where you can spread your books out, and that's in the kitchen. As Dad and Jen were having a drink and chatting in there, I didn't want to disturb them. Dad doesn't get to spend enough time with Jen as it is.

I looked around the tiny bedroom I shared with Emma and thought, I suppose I could put my books on the bottom bunk and sit on the floor to work. I wished Dad would buy the fold-down desk he'd promised, but he never seems to get around to it. Maybe I could work at Becca's instead, I thought. She's so lucky being an only child. She has a bedroom all to herself, plus her own computer and a desk unit with shelves. Maybe I'll give her a ring.

'I've been working on a song,' said Becca when she picked up the phone. 'It's a love ballad. Why don't I ring Jade and see if she wants to do some band practice and we could maybe put some music to the words?'

I wasn't really in the mood for Jade. She's Mac's younger sister and can be mega snotty. She's in Year Ten and thinks she knows it all as she's lived in London most of her life and tends to look down her nose at us as though we're country yokels. However, when Mac told her that Becca and I had a girl band, she asked if she could join us and I have to admit, she has got a brilliant voice.

In the rest of the house, there was a battle of sounds between Em banging on the piano downstairs, the telly blasting out and Luke playing Eminem next door. I looked at my books strewn all over the bed. No peace here, I thought.

'Good idea,' I said. 'I'll meet you at yours.'

I put my school stuff away and quickly got changed into my combats, T-shirt and leather jacket then headed down-stairs for the back door.

'Where do you think you're going?' said Dad.

'Um, Becca's. We've got a school project we're working on.'

Luckily, Dad was in a good mood so didn't object. 'Make sure you're back at a reasonable hour,' he said as I shut the door behind me.

As I cycled over to Becca's, there was a strange feeling in the pit of my stomach. Jen's words from earlier that evening were nagging me. Honesty is the best policy she'd said and, although she was applying it to Squidge, I couldn't help but think I hadn't been honest with Dad just now. I'd told a lie. He wasn't too enthusiastic about the band idea, so lately, whenever we got together, I didn't give him all the details. A white lie. That's what I'd told. Was that OK? It wasn't harming anyone. Or was it? This truth versus lying business is beginning to get to me, I thought, as I peddled furiously up the hill to Becca's house.

As soon as I got to Becca's, she took me up to her room and insisted on reading me her latest song. She fancies herself as a songwriter and I've haven't the heart to tell her that her lyrics are truly, spectacularly *awful*.

'Ready?' she asked as I took off my jacket and flopped on her bed.

'Ready,' I said, bracing myself for inevitable. Then I thought, no, give her a break, maybe this time she'll prove me wrong.

She rummaged around the usual debris on her desk and found her piece of paper and began to read.

I met a boy around about, Ollie is his name.
The way he looked so cute and cool crawled right into
        my brain.
I'm sure that since that moment I've never felt quite right,
And when someone called him a flash git, I got
        into a fight.
When I see him I'm happy and squishy and warm,
'Cause I think Ollie's the coolest boy ever to be born.
One day I'll walk right up to him and tell him who I am,

Then he'll say that he fancies me without a doubt,
And how about next Friday, can we go out?

'What do you think?' Becca said expectantly.

'Um, maybe the end needs some polishing?' And the beginning and the middle, I thought.

'There's more,' she said. 'There's a chorus.'

Oh no, I thought. Like I'm ever going to sing this. In public.

'Ollie, Ollie, you're my brolly,' she read. 'My cover when it rains. Ollie, Ollie, I'm off my trolly, You've scrambled up my brains.'

I was dying to laugh but made my face go straight. 'Hmmm. Interesting,' I said as a voice in my head questioned, now was that a half-truth, white lie, or an outright fib?

Just at that moment the doorbell rang downstairs. 'That'll be Jade,' I said. 'Let's see what she thinks.'

Jade burst in a moment later. As always, she was looking fab in a mini hipster denim skirt and a short asymmetric T-shirt which showed off her flat tummy and the diamante stud through her belly button.

'Don't you ever tidy up?' she asked as she cleared a space on the floor where she could sit.

'I like it like this,' said Becca. Her room was always a mess and, this evening no less than usual, there were books, magazines, clothes and shoes all over the place. 'Us creative types haven't time for being anally retentive about tidiness.'

Hah. That put her in her place, I thought, as Jade moved a sock and pulled a face like she'd touched a piece of dog poo.

'I've written a new song,' said Becca, ignoring Jade's expression and beginning to read the lyrics.

Poor Becca, I thought, she's in for it now.

'Is that Ollie as in Ollie Axford?' asked Jade when Becca had finished.

'Yes,' said Becca. 'Why, do you know him?'

Jade smiled coyly and tossed her long blond hair back over her shoulder. 'Might do.'

Becca looked freaked. 'Er, you weren't with him the other day down on Cawsand beach, were you?'

'No,' said Jade. 'Why?'

'Nothing,' said Becca.

'So why ask? What's going on?'

I picked up one of Becca's books from the floor and made like I was really interested in it, but the words on the page were swimming before my eyes. Please don't ask me anything, I prayed. I don't want to go through it all again.

'Nothing,' said Becca. 'Just his sister Lia is a friend of ours and she said he was snogging some local girl on the beach last week.'

'Really? We must find out who it was,' said Jade. 'But it doesn't necessarily mean anything. A boy like Ollie is bound to have girls queuing up for him.'

'And are you one of them?' said Becca looking daggers at her.

'Might be. Why, are you?'

'Might be,' said Becca.

Ooooh, I thought. This is getting more and more complicated.

Cinders

LIA PHONED on Saturday morning just as I was cleaning the bathroom.

'Do you want to come over?' she asked. 'Mum's got a few friends down and they've all gone off horse-riding and I'm bored.'

'Can't,' I sighed. 'Saturday's for doing chores.'

Lia sounded disappointed. 'But Becca's coming. See if you can come later.'

I put the phone down and saw that Jen was standing behind me. 'Who was that?' she asked.

'Lia Axford,' I said. 'Invited me over. But I haven't finished the bathroom yet, then I've – '

Jen put her hand on my shoulder and squeezed it. 'Leave it with me, Cinders. You shall go to the ball.'

Half an hour later I was on my way over to Lia's. Jen had been brilliant. She had a word in Dad's ear and, amazingly, he agreed to let me go. A whole day without jobs. Hurray.

I wish she'd move in permanently, I thought – life would be fantabulous. I can tell Dad's worried about how I and the others would take it, but we'd love it. I tried to talk to him about it a couple of weeks ago, but he changed the subject mucho fast. It's a shame because we all really like Jen and want him to be happy but, when I tried to tell him, he murmured something about us being his responsibility, then he went off to the shop.

All this thinking I've been doing about truth and being honest lately, it applies to me and Dad as well. It's not that we're dishonest with each other exactly, more like we don't tell the whole truth. One day we need to sit down and have a proper talk about things, I decided. Some day when I can get him on his own.

It was a cloudless blue sky as I peddled up and over towards Millbrook and it felt like the clear air was blowing away some of the cobwebs in my head. There's the truth, I thought, then white lies, then half-truths, then fibs. Then there's good and bad lies, some to protect, some to keep the peace and some that are plain cowardly, I suppose. Like when I've told Dad I've been somewhere I haven't so he won't be mad – like saying I've been at an extra class at school when actually I've been out spacing with Bec. Which is best, I wondered, and what do *I* do? Am I an honest person or a fibber?

I decided to keep an account over the next week of every fib or white lie that I told, starting tomorrow.

After ten minutes, I'd left Millbrook behind and reached Barton Hall. But how was I was going to get in? The imposing wrought iron gates in front of me were firmly shut. I spied a small intercom box on one of the adjacent pillars and pressed the buzzer.

A camera whizzed into action and took a look at me. I smiled hopefully.

'Hi Cat, come on up,' said Lia's voice through the intercom, then I heard a buzz and, as if by magic, the gates began to open.

As I cycled up, down and around the bends of the long drive, I began to feel apprehensive. Although I'd been here before with Dad, someone had come down to collect the box of groceries at the gate. This time I was going inside as a guest. At least Ollie wasn't there. That *would* have been too much.

It seemed to take ages cycling up to the house, past stables, outhouses and an endless wood. I was just starting to think I was lost when suddenly the trees opened up and I saw Lia and Becca waiting for me at the top of the drive with two red setters running around their feet.

The house was very grand, like an old hotel, nestling in amongst a wooded area at the back and sides and, in front, there was a terraced lawn lined with huge palms in ginormous pots.

'Wow, Cat, you have got to see this place,' beamed Becca as I got off my bike and was immediately accosted by the dogs, who greeted me like their oldest, dearest friend. 'It's totally amazing. They've got their own tennis courts and a swimming pool *and* a billiards room.'

'This is Max and Molly,' said Lia. 'Down, good dogs, down.' Max jumped down, but Molly seemed to have taken a liking to me and had my sleeve firmly in her teeth. 'Down, Molly, down. Sorry Cat, she's still young and gets over-excited when people arrive.'

'Er, no prob,' I said as Lia prised her off. I leaned my bike against the porch and looked at the cars parked to the side of the house. A gleaming silver Mercedes, a black BMW and a Range Rover. 'Chauffeur was busy so I came on my own transport,' I laughed.

Lia smiled shyly. Do you want to come in? I'll give you the grand tour. That is, if Becca doesn't mind seeing it all again.'

'No, course not,' said Becca.

We followed her into the porch and through a door, which opened up into a hall with high ceilings and large mirrors and a wide staircase.

'This is the drawing room,' said Lia leading me into an elegant room with an enormous bay window and lovely thick curtains right down to the floor. Through the window was the most stunning view of the lawns in front leading down to the sea.

'They have their own private beach down there,' said Becca, who was clearly enjoying herself immensely. 'And boats.'

As I followed them round room by room, I began to enjoy myself as well. I felt like a tourist going round one of those National Trust stately homes. I'd never seen anything like it except for a hotel last year when my Auntie Brenda got married. Every downstairs room (four living rooms!) had lovely comfortable furniture, open fireplaces with baskets of logs next to them, and everywhere there were what looked like expensive antiques. Best of all, though, each room had its own television. Upstairs, all of the bedrooms (eight!) had their own bathroom and even some of *them* had televisions.

'It must be a dream to live here,' I said. 'Not having to share a bedroom or a bathroom and having your very own telly must be heaven.'

'Well I hope you'll come and stay some time,' said Lia. 'Mum loves having people over.'

'Yes please,' I said as she led us down a corridor and into another bedroom.

'This is where our Cornish Casanova lives,' she said.

'Ollie's room,' said Becca and gave me a wicked grin behind Lia's back.

It felt strange looking at his private things. There were loads of photos of him and his friends and family and seeing them made my insides go funny. Get back in your box, I told the thoughts in my head. I wasn't going to hang about in there, but Becca was busy scanning his shelves, his books, his CDs.

She grinned. 'Research'. Then looking at Lia, she said to me, 'It's OK, I told her I've seen Ollie about and really fancy him. Lia knows all my secrets now.'

Typical Becca. She wears her heart on her sleeve and can never keep anything to herself for long.

Lia smiled back at her. 'Don't say I didn't warn you, though.'

For a moment I felt a twinge of jealousy. Not because of the beautiful house or anything. I was jealous because it used to be so open between Bec and I. No secrets. And now she was sharing secrets with Lia. I hated not being able to tell her everything that was happening to me. It was like an invisible wall had gone up and I was stuck behind it.

We spent the rest of the afternoon doing the 'grand tour', but even after two hours, we still hadn't seen all the grounds.

'You must come and do *le grand tour* of our house one day,' I laughed. 'It'll take less than five minutes. Three up, two down and a small bathroom.'

'You don't mind, do you?' asked Lia as we stopped at the top of the lawns.

'Mind what?' asked Becca looking puzzled.

Lia indicated the estate with a sweep of her hand. 'All this.'

'Mind it? I *love* it,' I said.

'It's just, sometimes people are a bit funny about our family having so much, you know . . .'

'You mean jealous?' I asked.

Lia nodded. 'I hope it won't stop us being friends.'

'Course not,' I said. 'I mean, course I'm a bit jealous, who wouldn't be? But I was hoping you'd ask me and Bec to move in. No one would even notice we were here. We could camp out in one of the stables with the horses.'

Lia laughed and looked relieved. 'Good, then let's go and ask Meena to get us something to drink.'

'Who's Meena?' asked Becca.

Lia looked embarrassed. 'Our housekeeper. Sorry.'

As we followed her back into the house and into a kitchen that was bigger than our whole house put together, I couldn't help but think that people are strange. Here's Lia, who has everything: looks, glam parents, an enormous house and housekeeper, her own bedroom, bathroom, telly and goodness knows what else, and yet she's worried that *we* wouldn't want to be friends with her. Then I realised the one thing she *didn't* have down here was friends and that's what makes anywhere more enjoyable, whether you're in a huge place like this, or in a tiny place like where I live. You learn fast when some-one like your mum dies that it's people that count. Friends. I looked at her with increasing admiration. She had it all but wasn't the least bit stuck up, unlike Jade, who acts as though she's God's gift. Friends. That's what's important, I thought, and Lia obviously knows that. I hoped we would be friends. And I hoped Becca and I would go back to the way we used to be. If only I could tell her the truth.

Liar, Liar, Pants on Fire

Sunday: Fibs (1)

Went to Plymouth with Squidge, Lia, Becca and Mac. Lied that I was fifteen to get into the movie. Well *everyone* does that, don't they? Lia and Becca did as well so don't feel too bad.

Monday: Fibs (2)

Was late for school. Said bus didn't show up, when actually I missed it because Emma refused to go to school in her polka dot knickers, as she said you could see the dots under her pink trousers. She made such a fuss that I had to find her another pair, which made me late. Not my fault and no way I'm explaining all *that* to Mrs Jeffries.

Becca asked if a spot on her nose was obvious. Said no, when actually it was ginormous.

Tuesday: Fibs (3)

Ohmigod! Lied to Becca again, as she'd rewritten her love ballad and it was worse than the first version. Didn't want to hurt her feelings, so said it was cool.

Lied to Dad. He was working late and we got out a horror video from the shop, but told him we'd watched Disney's *Aladdin*.

Lied to Squidge when he asked if he could come over. I said I had homework to do, when actually I'd finished it and wanted to watch the horror movie with Luke, Joe and Emma. Felt mean after, because Squidge loves horror movies.

Wednesday: Fibs (0)

Hurrah.

Thursday: Fibs (5)

Eep. Eep.

Lied for Luke. A drippy girl at his school called Josephine Talbot has got a crush on him and he can't stand her. When she phoned, he asked me to say he wasn't in. And I did.

Lied to some Bible bashers who came to the door and asked if I was at peace with my God. Told them we were all Devil worshippers in our house to get rid of them. Joe and Luke thought it was hilarious and would have put on last year's Hallowe'en masks that drip blood and followed them down the street if I hadn't stopped them.

Lied to someone who phoned while we were having supper. He wanted to drop in next week and redesign our kitchen for free. Could *not* get him off the phone, so told him we were a hippie family and lived in a wigwam and cooked on a barbecue. Dad thought it was hilarious, so now I'm getting support on all sides for fibbing.

Lied to Becca, as she asked me about Ollie *again*.

Lied to Becca, after she saw Jade talking to me on the way into school. Jade was slagging Becca off and saying she never stood a chance with Ollie. When Bec asked what we were talking about, I said, 'Oh about herself as usual'.

Friday: Fibs (3)

Half-lied to Mr Ford in physics and said that I hadn't done my homework because our computer had run out of cartridge ink and I hadn't had time to go to Plymouth to get any. Was a half-lie, because the real reason was that Dad couldn't afford it this week and I didn't want to say that in front of the whole class and have everyone feeling sorry for me.

Lied to Moira Ferguson when she invited me to her party on Sunday. Said my cousins were coming to stay for the weekend. I can't stand her – she's so bossy.

Lied to Dad that I had done my music practice, when actually I haven't even looked at the piano in weeks.

Saturday: Fibs (1)

Lied when my gran phoned and asked if I liked the
sweater she'd sent that she knitted herself. Told her I
loved it, but really it is hideous.

I am appalled at myself. I always considered myself to be
an honest person, but I am the Fibbing Fibster of Fibville.
I wished I could talk to someone about it, but most people
would think I was mad or a criminal or something. I
wished Mum were here. I went into my wardrobe, found
my secret box and unlocked it. I kept all my special things
in there: old photos, cards Squidge had sent me and some
stuff of Mum's – a letter from her, bits of her old jewellery
and a bottle of Mitsouko by Guerlain. When we finally
cleared her stuff out of the cupboards in Dad's room, I
found the perfume and hid it. Whenever I smelt it, it
brought her back like she was in the house somewhere. I
took the cap off and did a spray on to my wrist and sniffed.
As always the soft flowery scent made me think of her.
What would she have made of all this and her daughter
qualifying for the Teenage Fibber of the Week award? She
was always so honest herself. All through her illness, she'd
insisted on knowing exactly how she was and also on
telling us the truth about her condition. I heard her telling
Dad once that she didn't want to give us false hope and
that death was a part of life and not to be shunned. She was
so brave about it all and I'm glad I knew how bad things

were because I think she was right: it would have been even worse if she'd just disappeared one day and I hadn't known how ill she'd really been.

Dad popped his head in the door. 'Supper's ready, Cat.'

I quickly stuffed my box back in the wardrobe as I didn't want him to see me getting upset, but he didn't go straight away. His eyes had misted and he seemed to be looking for someone else in the room. I think he'd smelled the Mitsouko. Maybe now was the time to have that talk about things, I thought. We'd never really sat down and talked about Mum's death, just the two of us.

'You all right, Dad?' I asked.

He coughed then sort of sniffed the air again. 'Yes fine. Just . . . I thought . . . oh, nothing.'

Then he left before I could say anything else.

Before I went down to supper, I got out Mum's letter to me. She'd written it a few weeks before she died and asked Dad to keep it and give it to me the day I started secondary school. It said:

My darling girl,

    All grown up and ready to start a new school and how I wish I was going to be there to see it. I wanted to write to you and tell you how proud I am of you. You have been a strength to me over the last year and the light of my days. Be strong, Cat. Be true to yourself

and always be brave as I know you will be.
God bless. My love will always be with you

Your mum.

That's it, I thought. From now on I am going to reform and
be brave just like Mum was. From now on, I'm going to
tell the Absolute Truth.

The Absolute Truth

I STARTED the new week feeling bright and optimistic.
Pure as the newly fallen snow, that was going to be me.

Monday: Truths (2)

On the bus going to school, Becca asked what I thought
of her latest song. I told her to stick to dancing.

She's not speaking to me.

At home after school, Josephine Talbot phoned for Luke.
He was in front of me waving his arms madly and
mouthing, 'No, *nooooo*.' But being a truth teller, I told her
he was there and handed him the phone.

Luke's not speaking to me.

Tuesday: Truths (1)

At school, when Mr Ford asked where my homework was,
I told him I hadn't done it. Then he asked why not, so I
told him that a new series of 'Dawson's Creek' had started

and after that I felt tired and couldn't be bothered as it was *sooo* boring.

Got detention. But am the class hero.

Wednesday: Truths (2)

Bec's speaking to me again, but the spot on her nose has grown even bigger than last week. When she asked if I was sure it wasn't noticeable, I told her that actually, it looked like it had taken over half her face.'

She's not speaking to me again.

Bit of a do at home this evening. Dad was going down the video shop and asked what we wanted. Emma said, *'Jeepers Creepers'*. Then Dad said, 'But we don't watch horror in this house *do* we?'

I didn't have to tell the truth this time as Emma reeled off a whole list of videos that we've watched when Dad's been out.

Am in the doghouse.

Thursday: Truths (2)

At school break, Mac asked if I thought he stood a chance with Becca. I said, no as she's so in love with Ollie Axford that no one else even gets a look in. It's the truth.

Mac went off in a sulk.

In second break, Lia asked if I fancied Ollie. Didn't know what to say at first, but as it's my truth week, I knew I had no choice and admitted I did. Turns out she knew I was 'the girl on the beach'! I was amazed because I thought he hadn't ever mentioned my name, but apparently he'd phoned from London and asked Lia if she'd met me and told her that I was the girl he had been with in Cawsand. She also said she had guessed I liked Ollie because I go mega-quiet whenever anyone talks about him. Interesting. Seems that sometimes you can't hide what you really feel.

V. glad I told her the truth. She'd never have trusted me again if I'd lied. I had to beg her not to tell Becca, though, as I want to pick my moment and don't want to hurt her. She agreed and said that Ollie has asked after me and she thinks he really likes me!! Plus he's coming down next weekend and he's going to go to Rock with a few mates. Arghhh.

So far this week, thank God, thank *God*, Becca hasn't asked about him.

Friday: Truths (4) Excellent!

On the school bus, Moira Ferguson asked how last weekend went with my cousins. Tricky one, but I was brave – I was the Truth Teller of Torpoint. I told her that they didn't come and, anyway, I wasn't in a party mood.

Later, Moira told the whole class that I am a liar. Phff. She obviously doesn't realise that I am She Who Is Honest.

At home in the evening, Gran phoned and asked if I'd

worn my new sweater. I finally admitted I hadn't as it just wasn't me. It was awful, as she went very quiet and asked to speak to Dad. He gave me a lecture about being diplomatic. It's not easy to be diplomatic *and* tell the truth.

In the doghouse again.

Later that evening, the Bible bashers came back to ask if I was at peace with my God. I said I didn't know and invited them in for a half-hour of debate. Got told off for letting strange men in the house by Dad and told off by Joe and Emma for giving them the last of the chocolate chip cookies.

At supper that night, someone phoned to ask if we needed a new bathroom. I told him truthfully that yes, we did. Desperately. Then he said that his company would have a designer in our area next week who could come and give us a free quote and design. I told him that that would be great, but there's no way we could afford a new bathroom so it might be a waste of time. OK, he said, good night then.

Well *that* one was easy!

Saturday: Truths (1)

At the cinema in Plymouth, when the lady behind the kiosk asked how old I was, I told her: fourteen. Course she wouldn't let me in. Then she looked at Becca, who promptly lost her nerve and now Becca's not very happy with me. She phoned an hour after I got home and said

I'd been acting really weird and what was the matter with me this week. I told her that I'd decided to tell the truth, the whole truth and nothing but the truth, so help me God. She said not to bother and that she wanted the old Cat back.

By the end of the week, I felt more confused than ever. Telling the truth is supposed to be the right thing to do, I thought, but it doesn't always work out. However, I wasn't ready to give up yet.

On Sunday Mr Squires drove me and Squidge to Rame Head, as he had to fix a car that had broken down in the car park up there. While he worked, I went up to the Head with Squidge. To tell The Truth.

Rame Head is my favourite place in all the peninsula, a little hill jutting out over the sea with a tiny Druid church on top. The local hippies all say that very powerful lay lines converge there. Don't know about that, but it does feel good up there. All you can see for miles on either side is sky and ocean.

'Squidge?' I said after we'd sat for a while gazing out over the view.

Squidge looked over and smiled. 'What?'

I was determined to do it this time. Absolute Truth. Being brave, that was me.

'Just, er, do you think, maybe it's time we moved on . . .'

He leapt up. 'Yes, it is getting chilly, quite a wind has blown up. Here, have my fleece.'

He picked up my bag and set off down the hill.

Try again, I thought as I followed him.

'Er, Squidge. You know I really like you, don't you?'

He grinned. 'And I like you.'

'Well I was thinking maybe we could reassess our relationship.'

'Already have,' he said cheekily. 'I get five stars, you get three.'

I had to laugh. 'I mean, don't you ever fancy other girls?'

He shook his head. 'Nope. Though that Lia's pretty stunning.'

D'oh? That wasn't part of the script and it threw me for a minute. 'So are you saying you fancy her?'

'No.'

'But you find her stunning?'

'Yes.'

He came back up a few steps and put his arm round me. 'You never need to feel insecure with me, Cat. You and me have something special. Must be your old hormones playing you up.'

I smiled at the familiar line as Squidge took my hand and, looking at me earnestly, said, 'What we have, it's on another level.'

I giggled, as we were halfway down the hill by now – another level.

'Like we can always be straight with each other, you know?' he continued.

I nodded, determined to see it through, 'Yeah, mainly. Best of friends. Though sometimes it's hard to find the right words to say what you mean.'

Squidge ran down the last steps ahead of me and into the field that led back to the car park. Then he did a sort of mad Indian dance. 'The right words? What like I'm the best-looking boy in the school. And brilliant. And cool. And *soooo* modest.' Then he ran the rest of the way back to the car.

Yeah, I thought, all of that. 'Plus I want to finish with you,' I said, but he was too far ahead to hear and the words got blown away in the wind.

Rockin' in Rock

'N.O. NO.'

'But Dad,' I said, 'I've done all my jobs *and* my home-work. Everyone's going. Pl*eeease*.' I really *really* wanted to go. I wanted a day out with the girls. A day off from truth and lies. A day away from it all.

'Who's everyone?'

'Becca, Lia, Jade.'

'Is Squidge going or Mac?'

'No, they have footie on a Saturday afternoon. But Becca's dad is going to pick us up.'

'And how were you going to get there? I can't take you.'

'Bus. There's one leaving at three.'

Dad shook his head. 'I've heard about Rock. Teenagers get up to all sorts there. Sex, drugs, drink.'

'Dad, I'm *fourteen*, not a little girl any more. You can trust me. We only want to go and have a look around. And Becca's dad . . .'

'I heard you the first time. He'll pick you up. I don't know, Cat. There may be lots of older boys there just waiting for girls like you lot to turn up.'

Oh I *hope* so, I thought.

'If Squidge was going to keep an eye on you, I might think about it,' continued Dad.

No way was I inviting Squidge. This was to be a girls' day out, but then I remembered that Lia had said that Ollie was going.

'Lia's brother will be there.'

'How old is he?'

'Um, seventeen, I think.'

Dad seemed to be weakening. 'And will he be with your lot or off with his own crowd?'

'Oh, let her go, Peter,' said Jen who had been listening in from the hall. 'If this older boy's going to be there, they'll be fine.'

The bus got into the car park at Rock just after four. We'd all put on our make-up on the bus and were in major project mood – finding some boys. Luckily, Becca had put my behaviour of the last week down to hormones and had forgiven me for telling her the truth. She looked stunning. This was her 'big day'. She'd been looking forward to meeting Ollie for weeks and she'd spent the whole morning blow-drying her hair straight until it shone like red silk. She and Lia looked like Rose Red and

Rose White as they gave their long hair a final brush, then got off the bus.

'Do I look all right?' asked Becca, pulling down her tank top. 'Maybe I shouldn't have worn this. I look enormous. I should have worn my blue top.'

'Becca,' I said. 'You look fab. Relax.' She was always the same. Ever since I've known her she's had a thing about being too big. As if. She's a typical case of wanting to be Kate Moss when actually she's more like Kate Winslet. No one's ever happy, I thought. I wished I was tall and curvy like her, she wished she had straight hair like mine.

'Right, let's assess the situation,' she said looking around at the mass of cars. 'Beach or café?'

'Beach,' said Lia. 'Best make the most of it before it gets dark. I said we'd meet Ollie at the Mariner's Arms at about six-thirty.'

'Ollie. Cool,' said Jade and started off along the narrow path that led through gorse bushes down to the sea. Becca made a face behind her and Lia and I laughed. This was going to be interesting, I thought. Jade and Becca fighting over Ollie. Not me, of course, I was completely cool about him. Sort of.

We decided to wander down the beach, then pick a good place to sit and watch the world go by. It was crowded for October but then, I suppose, everyone wanted to make the most of what might be the last nice day before autumn set in. There were people having picnics and watching the boats, others playing frisbee, kicking balls about, and others walking dogs. A ferry had just arrived from Padstow on the other side of the bay and groups of teenagers made their way down the gang plank on to the beach then surveyed the scene, like us, looking for the talent.

Lia smiled. 'I think I may have to go and have a swim.'

'Are you mad?' I asked. She was fully clothed and even though it was a bright day, there was a chill wind, far too cold for stripping off.

'Ah gotya,' said Jade. 'A *definite* ten out of ten.'

I looked over to where they were staring and there was a gorgeous boy in a wet suit, sitting with a pair of binoculars.

'I may have to go and drown,' laughed Jade. 'That life guard is divine.' She minced up the beach near where he was. 'Oh save me, *save* me, I'm drowning.'

'I wish she would,' said Becca, as the boy looked over at Jade then turned back to sea with a bored expression as though he'd seen it all before.

After our walk up and down, Jade spotted a group of lads sitting beside one of the boats.

'They look like a laugh,' she said. 'Let's go and sit near them.'

Lia glanced over, then shook her head. 'I don't think so.'

But Jade ignored her and went and sat down near the boys. She went into her hair tossing routine interspersed with flirty looks in their direction.

There were four boys and they seemed to be playing

some sort of game. They had loads of cans of lager and a plump boy was counting on a stopwatch then, every thirty seconds or so, he'd fill everyone's glasses and they'd all knock back their drinks.

As he gulped down the liquid in his glass, he noticed Jade doing her routine.

'The idea is to drink as much as possible without going for a whaz,' he said in a very posh but slurred voice.

'Oh very clever,' said Becca.

'We're Rupert, *hic*, Baz, Henry and Patrick,' said a blond boy pointing at each of them in turn.

'Which one's hic again?' I asked Lia.

'Jade, Lia, Becca and Cat,' said Jade, who seemed blind to the fact that these boys were drunk out of their skulls.

'What school do you go to?' asked Rupert.

'Ignore them,' said Lia as Baz got up and came to sit in front of her. His eyes were completely out of focus as he gazed at her. 'Hey, you're *gorgeous*,' he dribbled. 'Up for a bit of snoggage?'

Henry got up and came over to sit next to me. As he leaned close, his breath stank of booze and I had to lean back to get away from the fumes. He propped himself up against me and pointed upwards. 'The stars are in the sky, Cat,' he drooled. 'Lie back, put your head on my shoulders and I'll show you Uranus.'

'Let's go,' I said, pushing him off then getting up and walking towards the slope that led to the cafés.

'Cat, *Cat*,' called Henry. 'Don't go. Be my honey.'

'What a load of plonkers,' said Becca, getting up and coming over to join me. 'Let's get away from them.'

Lia got up but Jade seemed reluctant to move. In the end she had no choice but to get up as well, as we were all walking away.

'Come to our beach party later,' called Baz as we backed off. 'Polzeath Beach, you only need some alcohol or a pair of breasts to get in.'

They all started sniggering, then Rupert suddenly looked as if he was going to be sick. He crossed his legs and dashed behind a boat. 'Have to whaz, have to whaz *now* . . . ahhhhhh.'

'Boys can be *really* stupid,' said Lia. 'Sometimes I wonder why we bother.'

'Ah, but then a special one comes along,' said Becca. 'What time did you say we're meeting Ollie?'

'Six-thirty-ish,' said Lia.

'You lot are such a load of killjoys,' said Jade catching us up. 'They were only having a laugh.'

Lia looked back at them. 'Nah. I know boys like that from my old school. They're all the same, like cardboard cut outs. They even dress the same, like some kind of uniform: brown loafers, brown belt, chinos and a Ralph Lauren or Tommy Hilfiger top.'

I glanced back. She was right. They were all dressed the same.

Jade had gone into a sulk. 'I thought they made a refreshing change from the usual pond life at our school.'

'You were wasting your time,' said Lia. 'Their motto is, Life and Lager.'

We walked along the road towards the pub. There was a group of older boys sitting on a wall and I couldn't help but notice that they all had the same uniform on as well. Brown shoes, brown belt, chinos. One of them shook his head as we walked past.

'Too young, too young, too young,' he said sadly. He looked like he was drunk as well and a moment later, he fell backwards off the wall.

Outside the Mariner's Arms the pavement was heaving with teenagers. There must have been about fifty standing about, laughing, drinking, eyeing each other up.

'Paradise,' said Jade perking up again as she surveyed the many groups of boys in the crowd. 'I'm home. Um, going to do a wreckie. Back later.' And with that, she disappeared.

Becca got out her mirror to reapply her lipstick. 'Ohmigod,' she shrieked. 'My *hair*. It's gone curly.'

Poor Becca. Her hair is the bane of her life. Personally I think it suits her curly, but she hates it and is forever buying new products and dryers to keep it straight. It's never any use, as the moment she steps out, especially if there's any moisture in the air like there is here, it coils back into its natural curls.

'Got to go and sort it before we see Ollie,' she said. 'I'm just off to find the Ladies. Don't do anything without me.'

We reassured her that we wouldn't, but already we could see boys eyeing us up and nudging each other.

'Excuse me,' said a dark haired boy sidling up to Lia, 'would you by any chance have a pair of knickers I could borrow?'

Lia looked taken aback, but I was intrigued; I hadn't heard this as a chat-up line before.

'Sorry,' said Lia. 'None spare.'

'Would you swop the ones you've got on with mine, then?' he asked as he began unzipping his fly.

'Get lost,' said Lia turning her back on him.

Then a boy came up to me. 'Have you got a twenty pence piece?' he asked.

I looked in my purse. 'Er, no . . . I've only got a pound coin.'

'Has to be a twenty pence,' he said, grinning.

'Why?'

'So I can call your dad and tell him you won't be home tonight.'

'Cat!' said a stern voice behind me. 'You *know* you're not allowed out of the detention centre without a guard!'

I turned and there was Ollie. 'You can leave now,' he said to the boy, 'before she has one of her turns and has to kill you.'

The boy scarpered and I laughed as Ollie smiled down at me.

'Hi Cat,' he said.

As always, he looked gorgeous. There were some pretty good looking boys in the crowd, but Ollie still stood out amongst them. Suddenly the atmosphere felt soft, like reality had melted at the edges. 'Hi,' I said.

At that moment, Becca reappeared on the steps of the pub. She went a brighter red than her hair when she saw Ollie and made her way through the crowd blushing like a bride walking towards the altar.

'Ollie, Becca, my friend,' said Lia. 'Becca, Ollie.'

Ollie smiled ravishingly at her. 'Anyone ever told you that you look like Nicole Kidman,' he asked.

He couldn't have said anything better. Nicole looks thinner than Kate Winslet. Becca was gone. Smitten. Knocked for six. Seduced.

'And I'm Jade,' purred Jade reappearing from nowhere and linking her arm through Ollie's. '*You* must be the *famous* Ollie Axford.'

11 White Lies and Barefaced Truths

THE JOURNEY back from Rock was a nightmare. Becca's dad picked us up at ten as arranged and Becca sat in the back and didn't say a word all the way home. She was furious with Jade, who had hogged Ollie from the moment she set eyes on him. He didn't seem to mind, though, in fact, he seemed to enjoy the attention. Later, when Bec's dad arrived, Jade declined the lift and cadged a ride back with Ollie instead.

Becca was almost hysterical at leaving them and we had to push her into the car, much to her dad's confusion.

Lia came with us although she was supposed to have gone back with Ollie. She didn't want to desert Becca and did her best to reassure her. Didn't do much good, though, as once we got in the car, Becca's lips were zipped.

The silence in the car was so uncomfortable I made an effort to lighten the atmosphere by chatting to Mr Howard, but underneath I couldn't help but feel jealous as well. Jealous that Ollie had played along with Jade. And jealous because he hadn't made more of a fuss of me. Some friend I am.

'It will all look better in the morning,' my mum used to say. After a while I decided to take her advice and snuggled up in the back of the car and fell asleep.

The phone was buzzing on Sunday.

'And did you *hear* the way she made her voice go all husky and deep when she was talking to him?' asked Becca.

'Probably nothing happened,' I said. 'They weren't totally alone, Ollie's mate was there and those other girls from London.'

'I know,' said Becca. 'I think that one called Tassie fancied Ollie as well.'

'So no worries. Jade had competition.'

'You've *got* to find out what happened, Cat. I can't bear to speak to her and have her gloat.'

'Haven't you spoken to Lia? She probably knows.'

'I'll phone you back,' said Becca. 'I'll call her now.'

Five minutes later Lia called.

'Bec's in a real state,' she said.

'I know. What happened? Did Ollie come home?'

'Yeah. About half an hour after us, so they can't have got up to much.'

'Didn't he say?'

'He's not up yet but, honestly, I don't think Jade's his type. Comes on too strong and Ollie prefers a bit of a challenge.'

'Do you think he liked Becca?'

'Hard to tell Cat. He flirts with everyone. I told you what he's like.'

'I know. Becca's really upset.'

'But what about you, Cat? How are you feeling about Ollie these days?'

'Dunno, really. More confused than anything.'

'Finished with Squidge yet?'

'No, but I'm going to do it soon.'

'Good. And Cat?'

'Yeah?'

'I want to talk to you about something. Not on the phone. One day at school when we're on our own.'

I was intrigued. What did she want to talk to *me* about?

At school on Monday, Jade was strutting round like the cat that got the cream. Not giving anything away, she smiled smugly over at us in assembly.

I cornered her at break in the playground.

'Um . . . what time did you get back on Saturday?' I asked, trying to keep my voice casual.

'Oh, Ollie dropped me off at about one.'

One? Lia said he got in not long after she did. Jade was clearly telling a fib.

'Had a good time, did you?' I asked.

Jade couldn't contain herself. 'He's asked me to the party.'

'What party?' I asked before I could stop myself.

'The one at the Axfords'. It's going to be the do of the year. Their dad's fiftieth or something. Why?' And now she *was* gloating. 'Didn't *you* know about it?'

'Er, I think Lia may have mentioned something.' I said. Stick to half-truths, I thought. Lia *had* mentioned wanting to talk to me about 'something', it was probably about the party. This was my new philosophy after last week's 'tell the truth' championships. A half-truth didn't cause half as much trouble and sometimes saved face. In this case, my face.

'I don't know why Becca even thinks she stands a chance with him,' continued Jade. 'In fact, he asked more about you than he did her. Are you sure you haven't met him before? You seemed pretty pally when he first came over.'

'Might have seen him about,' I said, though I was longing to ask what he'd said about me.

'Anyway, Becca's far too young for him. He clearly wants someone a bit more mature like *moi*.'

'You're only a year older than Bec,' I said, as I thought back to that day on the beach when I first met Ollie. He didn't seem to be bothered about age.

'Anyway, how do you know?' I asked. 'I actually know from a good source that age wouldn't put him off.'

Jade looked at me closely. 'What good source? Lia?'

'No, just someone I know.'

Jade nodded her head slowly as if something was dawning in her brain. 'Oh, I get it. I *thought* it looked as though he'd met you before Rock. You were that girl he was with in Cawsand weren't you? *Weren't* you? How else would he have known your name?'

I felt my cheeks colour. Bugger.

I didn't answer.

'And do Becca and Squidge know about your little adventure?' asked Jade.

'There's nothing to tell,' I blustered.

'Not by my book,' she laughed. 'I think there's a lot to tell and they'll be more than interested to listen.'

The Cat Is Out of the Bag 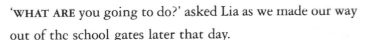 12

'WHAT ARE you going to do?' asked Lia as we made our way out of the school gates later that day.

'Don't know,' I said. 'Double don't know. Becca's still not got over Saturday night. This is all she needs.'

'Has Jade spoken to her?'

'Don't think so. Bec was with us all through lunch and her mum picked her up early from school to take her to the dentist, so I don't reckon Jade's got to her yet. Squidge though, I don't know about.'

There were loads of cars and parents blocking the road outside the school, but no sign of Lia's ride, so she came with me to the bus stop while I waited. In the traffic queuing to get out of the road, I noticed Jade and Mac in the back of their mum's battered old Daimler. Jade was gabbing on her mobile. She looked up as they drove past and she did a sort of royal wave then pointed at her phone. Oh bugger, I thought. I wonder who she's talking to. Squidge, Becca or taking out an ad in the local paper. I wouldn't put it past her. *Cat Kennedy caught in love scandal on Cawsand Beach.* Have you heard the latest?

'What do you think I should do, Lia?'

'Two things. You *must* talk to Squidge and Bec before Jade does. Call her bluff. And second, I think you should think seriously about what you want.'

'That's obvious isn't it? Not lose my two best mates. And not have them think that they can never trust me again.'

'I didn't mean that,' said Lia. 'I meant what do you want? *You.* Cat Kennedy.'

'What I want is last on the list at the moment.'

'Exactly,' said Lia, then she was quiet for a few minutes as if chewing over what she was going to say next. 'I know I've not known you long Cat, so tell me if you think I'm out of order . . . but this is what I wanted to talk to you about. It just seems to me that you *always* put yourself last on the list.'

'What do you mean?'

'I'm not saying it's a bad thing, in fact I really like the way you consider others and what they're going through. But I can't help but feel that you've got lost along the way somewhere. Like you think that you don't matter and everyone else does. I mean, who considers *your* feelings? What *you* want? Or need?'

Much to my surprise, my eyes filled with tears.

'Oh God, I'm sorry,' said Lia. 'Now I've blown it. Sugar. I didn't mean to make you . . . oh sugar sugar . . . I mean . . . what I meant is . . . you're stuck in a relationship that's gone stale. You want to move on, but you don't want to hurt Squidge, so you haven't told him. And you like Ollie, but you don't want to hurt Becca, so again, you sacrifice your feelings, so that everyone else can have a jolly time. I . . . I just think that sometimes, maybe you need to think about being true to *your* feelings instead of trying to protect everyone else's.'

She was right. I'd been so busy thinking about how the others would take the truth that I hadn't even thought about being true to myself. I blinked back the tears that threatened to spill down my cheeks. 'Must be mi old hormones playing me up,' I joked as I brushed my eyes.

'All I was trying to say, Cat, is that *you* matter too. You spend your whole life keeping the peace and making sure everyone else is all right, but it's always at your own expense.'

I felt my eyes filling up again. 'Sorry. Sorry. Don't be nice to me, don't be nice to me,' I said, covering my face with my hands.

Lia put her hand on my arm. 'But I *am* going to be nice to you, Cat. You've been a real mate to me since I came down here. And mates look out for each other.'

Just at that moment a silver Mercedes honked and Meena waved from the driver's seat.

'Here's my ride,' said Lia. 'Can we drop you? I'd feel rotten leaving you like this.'

I shook my head. 'Bus'll be here in a sec. Honest. You go.'

Truth was, I wanted some time to think about what Lia had said, and work out what I was going to say to Bec and Squidge before Jade got to them.

'When I got home I picked up the portable phone from the hall and ran upstairs. Emma had arranged all her dolls on the lower bunk bed and was feeding them digestive biscuits.

'Oh Emma,' I said, 'there are crumbs everywhere. Can't you play with them downstairs?'

'Luke and Joe are down there,' she replied as she tried to force-feed one of the dolls. 'Open your mouth, bad doll.' When the doll wouldn't eat, she pulled its head off, crammed the biscuit in the body, then put the head back on. 'There, good girl, now your tummy's full.'

'You can't do that, Emma,' I laughed in spite of my misery. 'You wouldn't like it if someone tried that on you.'

'No. But that's because my head doesn't come off,' she said with a serious face. 'Joe tried to get it off, but it's stuck down.'

'Look Em, I need the room for a bit,' I said.

'S'my room too,' she said.

'But I need some privacy. I want to make a phone call.'

'I don't mind. I won't tell anyone.'

'Emma, pleeease.'

'Then use Luke and Joe's, they're watching telly,' said Emma.

Oh, what wouldn't I give for my own room, I thought, for the umpteenth time as I went into the boys' room.

Joe wasn't downstairs, he was doing his homework on the floor, so the boys' room was no good for a private conversation either. I turned around and headed for the bathroom.

'What's after space, Cat?' Joe called after me as I locked the bathroom door.

'More space,' I called back as I put a couple of towels in the bath, climbed in, then dialled Becca's number.

There was a knock on the door. 'What's after more space?' asked Joe's voice. 'I mean at the end of the universe?'

'I don't know. Go *away* . . . oh hi, no not you, Becca. It's Cat.'

'Uh-huh?' said a thick voice.

'You all right? Fillings? Bad? How was the dentist?'

'OK. Mouth's a bit numb.'

'Well that's OK,' I said, 'because I need to talk to you. All you have to do is listen. It's about Jade. You know that time in Cawsand with Ollie . . .'

'Oh, I know everything,' said Becca. 'She phoned already . . .'

My heart began to beat faster. 'Already . . . ?'

'Yeah. Still trying to stir it,' continued Becca. 'She's such a two-faced cow.'

'What did she say?'

'That you were with Ollie on Cawsand Beach a few weeks ago.'

'And what did you say?'

'That I already knew. Hah. That shut her up. She thought it was some big secret or something, and I was going to be really shocked. I told her to mind her own business and that I knew all about it because you'd already told me. I didn't tell her you were there chatting up Ollie as a favour though.'

'Was that all she said?'

'Yeah.'

I sighed with relief. So now Jade thought Becca knew it all, so hadn't mentioned that I was the girl Ollie had snogged. Phew. But maybe I'd better fill her in on the rest and hope she wouldn't hate me forever. At least half the truth, that being my new way of dealing with things.

'Becca?'

'Yeah?'

'About Ollie. I feel I wasn't altogether honest with you because actually, er, I do think he's attractive.'

'Yeah,' said Becca. 'You'd have to be blind or stupid not to. You're not saying you're after him are you?'

It was time to come clean. I took a deep breath and launched in, 'No, I'm not Becca. You bagged him first and I would never –'

'Oh, hold on Cat, there's someone on the other line. I'll call you back . . .'

I sat up and decided to tidy the shampoo bottles and jars around the bath while I waited. Luke, Joe and Emma always leave the tops off everything. It drives me mad. And they never put the soap back in the soap dish, so it turns to slime. Uck.

I was just rinsing Em's plastic duck when Becca rang again.

'Did *you* know about this?' she demanded.

'What, Bec? Know about what?'

At first she didn't say anything but, being Becca, she couldn't hold it in for long. 'I don't believe it . . .' she began.

'What? *What?*' Oh no, I thought, it must have been Jade on the other line and she'd told Bec the whole story about me and Ollie. Just as things were going so well and I was about to tell her myself.

'Jade phoned again,' said Becca.

Prepare to die, Cat Kennedy, I thought.

'Did *you* know about this party?' she continued.

'*Party?* Oh, yeah, sort of, Lia's dad's. Jade said Ollie had asked her.'

'Exactly,' said Becca. 'So why hasn't Lia asked *us?*'

'Well it's not her party, Bec. It's her dad's party,' I began in Lia's defence though I had to admit that the thought had occurred to me that maybe we would be asked. Especially now that Jade was going.

'She phoned just to rub it in that Ollie had invited her,'

said Becca. 'So I told her we already had invites.'

'You didn't.'

'I did. I'd *love* to go, Cat. And I'm sure it's only a matter of time. Lia's bound to invite us.'

I remembered what Lia had said earlier about being mates and stuff, so why hadn't she mentioned the party?

'OK, but maybe we should wait until we're asked properly before we go spreading it around that we're going.'

'OK,' said Becca, 'but she's bound to ask us.'

'Yeah,' I said. 'Bound to, and Bec?'

'Yeah?'

'I just wanted to say . . .'

'Oh. Hold on,' she said and the line went silent for a moment. 'Got to go, Cat. Mum's calling me down for supper. '

Then she hung up.

Cats in the Cupboard 13

AFTER SUPPER I went to find Dad in the back garden. When it was warm, he often went out in the early evening for a bit of quiet and to smoke one of his roll-ups. He was sitting on the bench under the apple tree at the bottom of the garden, so I decided to take him out a cup of coffee and keep him company for a while.

'Thanks, Cat, that's really kind of you,' he said taking the coffee.

I sat next to him on the bench and wondered how to start a conversation. Lia's questions had started me thinking. Now I wanted to know what *he* wanted: if he felt that he didn't matter because everyone else had to come first on his list. It can't be easy having four kids, I thought, and no wife to talk it all through with. At least when you have a partner, you can share the responsibility and you have each other to sympathise with and support when the going gets rough. I decided it must be quite lonely being my dad.

'What you thinking about, Dad?'

'Oh, nothing important. Shop stuff.'

'And, er . . . are you happy?'

'Happy? What kind of question is that, Cat?'

'It's a "how are you" type of question. I mean, do you ever get lonely?'

Dad sighed. 'Everyone has times when they're a bit lonely, Cat, but you just get on . . .'

'Well, I just wondered if you had anyone to talk to. I suppose there's Jen but she's only here once a month.'

'What's this about?'

'I just wondered how you were feeling about things. Mum's been gone over five years now and well, do you think Jen'll ever move in one day?'

'Well that's really not your business is it, Cat?' he said standing up. 'Not your concern at all.'

And with that he stomped off inside as if I'd said something really bad. I felt like I'd been shoved aside when I was only trying to be friendly. If I couldn't have a real talk with my own dad, then who could I talk to? Not my business he'd said. We'd have loads to talk about if only he'd open up, but he obviously didn't want to. Not my business.

We have a strange relationship, I thought, as I sat and watched the sky turn from blue to lavender to navy. We both skirt around what's really going on with half-truths that don't reveal the whole story. We keep it safe and on the surface, but there's a whole load of stuff underneath, I know there is, if we could only both be brave enough to open up and let what we really think and feel out. The real truth.

Eep! Let the real truth out! I remembered Squidge. Had Jade got to him yet? I better call him *quick*.

I ran back up to my private office in the bathroom and dialled Squidge's number.

'He's on his way over to see you, love,' said Mrs Squires. 'He had a phone call then left in a bit of a hurry.'

Oh sugar, I thought. This is it. Jade's called him and he's on his way over to confront me. The last thing I wanted now was a showdown. I felt like hiding away. My attempt to talk to Dad had made me feel rejected and I wasn't in the mood for more upset.

As I went into the landing hall, I heard someone knock on the back door. I flew down the stairs and found Luke.

'Luke, *Luke*. Squidge is at the door. Tell him I'm out.'

'Where are you going to be?'

'Er, when the going gets tough, the tough, er . . . hide in the cupboard under the stairs,' I said, diving into the cupboard and hiding behind a coat. I felt such a hypocrite. One minute thinking that Dad and I had to be brave enough to tell each other the truth. Then a moment later hiding because, while being brave is a good idea in theory, it's another thing in reality.

Squidge knocked again.

'Out. *Out*. Tell him I'm out,' I whispered through the coats.

'Yeah, yeah,' said Luke. 'I heard you.'

'Is Cat in?' I heard Squidge ask when Luke opened the door.

'Er, no,' said Luke.

'Well, do you know where she is? I have to speak to her.'

Luke hesitated then called back. 'What should I tell him now, Cat?'

I could *kill* him. I should have known he'd get me back for letting him down when Josephine Talbot phoned last week. Thirty seconds later the cupboard door opened, Squidge pulled aside the coats and burst out laughing. 'Cat! What on earth are you doing in here?'

I pulled him into the cupboard with me. 'No peace anywhere in this stupid house. Emma's in the bedroom, Dad's in the living room, Luke's in the kitchen and Joe's upstairs. I, er . . . came in here to get a bit of peace.' Half-true, I thought, as there's no way I'm telling him that I'm in there hiding from him.

Squidge didn't bat an eyelid. 'Cool,' he said and settled himself on the floor at the back of the cupboard next to the electric meter. 'I see Mogley likes it in here too.'

I hadn't noticed, but there was the cat curled up in an old shoebox.

'I came straight round as soon as I heard . . .' said Squidge, giving Mogley a stroke.

'Oh, so you've heard . . . ?'

'Yes . . . I guess Lia told you . . .'

'No, Jade told me. I was trying to tell you, Squidge . . . you know that day . . . What do you mean, Lia? Why should she tell me? Tell me what?'

'I'm so chuffed,' he said, his face lighting up.

'*Chuffed?*'

'Yeah. Lia called. You know . . . about the party?'

'*Party?*'

'Yeah.'

We were clearly having two separate conversations and I was getting confused. Had Lia invited him and not me or Becca? Why? I made myself take a deep breath. Get a grip, Cat.

'OK. You're chuffed. Chuffed is good. Now what about the party?'

'My first job, Cat. I have my *first* job. I've been asked to make a video of the party up at the Axfords'. Apparently Mrs Axford didn't want a stranger doing it as there will be loads of famous people there. And she didn't want to ask one of her friends as they wouldn't be able to just chill and enjoy themselves. Lia knows I'm into film and she thought of me and told her mum about me. But best of all, I'm to be paid.' His grin grew from ear to ear. 'Good money, Cat. I mean *good* money.'

'Ah.' The penny was beginning to drop. 'Enough to go on that film course?'

'Added to what I've saved, yes, enough to go on my film course.'

I sat down next to him and gave him a hug. 'Oh Squidge, that's top. I'm really, really pleased for you. And er, did Jade call?'

'Oh yeah, some crapola about you being on Cawsand Beach with Ollie. She was mega-miffed when I told her that it was history and I already knew.'

'How? How do you already know?'

'D'oh, Cat. I was *there*.'

'*There*? On Cawsand Beach? When I was with Ollie. I never saw you.' Ohmigod, I thought. What did he see?

'Keep up, Cat. No, not on *Cawsand* Beach. When we played Truth, Dare on *Whitsand* Beach. Remember? Last beach party of the summer? Becca dared you to go and chat Ollie up for her.'

'Oh right,' I said.

'You OK, Cat?'

'Yeah. Sort of. Why?' I laughed.

'I get the feeling that you've not really been listening.'

'Oh I have. Honest. But have you ever thought that people only ever hear what they want to hear no matter what you tell them?' Amazing, I thought. Jade had tried her darnest to stir it for me, but Becca and Squidge had only heard what they wanted to hear.

'Yeah. And see what they want to see,' said Squidge finding a torch in Dad's toolbox on the floor. He switched it on under his chin so that he looked like a ghoul. 'Wuh uh uh uh.'

We sat there under the coats seeing who could do the scariest face with the torch and chatting about everything the way we always have done. He was full of ideas for the video and what music he'd put it to and how he'd edit all the footage he planned to shoot, so that it would tell a story about the party.

So I don't feel mad passion for him, I thought, but I still care about him and we do have fun. I felt a pang of anxiety about having to have The Conversation when I finally say it's over. Watching him sitting there so comfortably, legs stretched out, stroking Mogley, I thought, he's been a part of my life for almost as long as I can remember. I don't want to lose him and I'm certainly not going to ruin the mood by finishing with him tonight. Once again, it wasn't the right time and, looking around, nor did the floor of the cupboard under the stairs seem the right place!

14 Cat-astrophy

'BECCA, CAT, wait up,' called Mac as we headed back through the school gates the following day.

'Have you heard about this party?' he said.

'Yes,' I said. 'Are you going?'

'Yeah. Sort of. In fact, my mum asked me to speak to you both. Remember I told you she used to do posh dinners and stuff for rich people when we lived in London.'

'Yeah,' said Becca. 'So what?'

'She's doing the catering. She's been asked to do the food for the Axfords'. For two hundred people! So she needs staff. She asked me to ask if you and Becca would be waitresses for the night. I'm going to do it. Fifty quid each. What do you think?'

'*Whadttt?*' Becca's jaw dropped. 'Does Jade know you're asking us?'

'Yes, in fact it was her that suggested you to Mum. Mum offered it to her as well but then, you know Jade. She's such a princess and waiting on people would be way beneath her. Besides I think she's got an invite. But hey, fifty quid for a night's work isn't bad and we'll get to see who's there and what's going on and everything.'

Becca looked as if she'd just found out she'd picked the winning lottery numbers but lost her ticket. 'Yeah. It will be great fun watching Jade swan round with Ollie and everyone having a top time while we slave in the kitchen. NOT.'

Mac looked puzzled. 'What's the prob? Fifty quid and it'll be a laugh. Jade said you'd be really into it.'

'I bet she did,' said Becca. 'She must have known I was fibbing when I told her that we had invites. And now, I can just see it, she'll be all, "Oh, I've been invited and oh, *poor* you, having to work as a waitress. Just fetch me another drink will you?"'

'I could use the money, Bec,' I said. 'And perhaps I could accidentally on purpose throw one of the drinks all over Jade at some point.'

'I know how you feel sometimes,' Mac laughed. 'At least you don't have to live with her. So what shall I tell Mum? I said I'd let her know. Do you want to do it?'

'*We're* going to get *proper* invites,' said Becca. 'Lia is *our* friend.'

'So what shall I tell Mum?'

'Don't know yet,' I said watching Becca storm off to assembly. 'It's just going as waitresses wasn't quite the invite we'd been hoping for.'

* * *

Murphy's Law – Lia wasn't in assembly. Nor in class. Nor answering her mobile when Becca called for the fifth time when we got off the bus after school.

We went and sat on the wall at the top of Kingsand and Becca dialled again.

'Leave a message,' I whispered as Becca mimed, 'Voice mail', then hung up.

'Don't want to seem desperate,' said Becca. 'It would be awful if I went, so Lia where's our invites? And she had no intention of giving us one.'

'Maybe we have to let it go,' I said. 'It's not the end of the world.'

'Yes it is,' said Becca.

'You're right, it is. Two hundred people. It's going to be mega. Oh stinkbombs. Why is it never easy when you want something?'

Becca nodded. 'I think we have to face facts. I mean Jade's been asked. And Squidge has been asked. If Lia was going to invite us, she'd have called us, wouldn't she?'

'I guess. Maybe she only has a limited number and has invited mates from her old school.'

'Maybe she doesn't want us as mates after all. I mean, I suppose she does live in another world doesn't she? Maybe she thinks we'd show her up or something and are only fit to be there as waitresses. What do you think?'

I shrugged. 'I'd be disappointed. I really thought we

were friends, but hey, as Dad says, you get on . . . I've done waitressing before at do's in the village and it can be a bit of a laugh.'

'Well *I've* never been so insulted in my life,' said Becca. 'I don't think I could do it, not with Jade there.'

'OK, bottom line. No invite and go as a waitress? Or, no invite and miss the whole thing?'

'Well if you put it like that,' said Becca. 'I suppose those waitress outfits can look kind of sexy.'

Just at that moment, a loud honk attracted our attention. We looked up to see a turquoise metallic Ka slow down at the kerb in front of us. Ollie rolled down the window and waved.

'Here they are,' he said to Lia who was sitting in the passenger seat.

She leapt out and came over to where we were sitting.

'I've just come from your house, Becca,' she said. 'And I was just on my way to yours, Cat. I've been delivering these.'

She shoved a white envelope into my hand. It had my name written on it in beautiful handwriting. 'Yours is waiting at home for you, Becca. Invites to my dad's party. I was going to bring them to school today, then my horse had a fall this morning and I had to go to the vet with him to check he was OK . . .'

Ollie parked the car and got out to come and join us. 'I designed them,' he said proudly. 'Sorry yours are late, but

Mum's invited so many people we ran out of invites and had to get another lot done. They didn't arrive from the printers until today.'

I ripped open the envelope and laughed at what was inside. It was a card. On the front was a photo of a crystal whisky tumbler, but instead of there being whisky and ice in the glass, there was a pair of false teeth and ice. Underneath it said, *'Help me celebrate being fifty'*. On the back were all the details and the date and address.

'And your dad approved this, did he?' I asked.

Ollie nodded. 'I'd like to do design or advertising when I leave school.' He stood behind me and looked over my shoulder. S'cool isn't it?'

I nodded, lost for words. I was only aware of the proximity of him, breathing softly on my neck.

'So will you come?' asked Lia.

'Course,' said Becca looking straight at Ollie, who went over to her and put his arm round her. She went bright red and, like me, suddenly looked lost for words.

'And you, Cat. Will you come?' he asked.

'Course,' I said. 'If my dad will let me.'

'Oh, practise a song,' said Lia. 'We always have a talent hour when anyone who wants can get up and do whatever they want. I thought it would be a brilliant chance for your band to show off.'

'What band?' asked Ollie.

'We're called Diamond Heart,' said Becca.

'Nice name,' said Ollie.

'Cat thought of it,' said Becca suddenly finding her tongue. 'We mainly sing to backing tracks but sometimes I write lyrics.'

Oh God, I thought suddenly remembering the last lot she wrote: *Ollie, Ollie, you're my brolly, my cover when it rains.*

'Diamond Heart,' said Ollie. 'I'll put it on Mum's list. She's doing a sort of programme so everyone knows when they're on.'

Then he looked deeply into my eyes. 'I look forward to seeing you perform,' he said meaningfully.

Fairy Godmother

'WHAT ARE you doing?' asked Emma, on finding me with my head in the wardrobe and every item of clothing I owned strewn across the floor.

'Disaster, Em,' I said. 'I've been invited to a party and haven't got anything to wear. I need something really special.'

Emma curled up on the bottom bunk. 'You need a fairy godmother. Like Cinderella.'

'Don't happen to know one, do you?'

Emma shook her head, then went to one of her drawers and picked out a tiny blue leotard. 'You can borrow this if you like.'

'Thanks, Em, but I think it's a *bit* small.'

Both Becca and Lia had offered to lend me something of theirs and I'd had a session at both their houses going through their clothes, but nothing fit. When I tried their things on, they looked borrowed. Becca's five foot six and

114

I'm five foot two. Her dresses hung on me. Same with Lia, she's five foot five, willowy with hardly any chest, so her clothes were too tight on my top and too long on the bottom. I was beginning to think it would be easier to go as a waitress after all.

'What about your sparkly silver top?' asked Emma. 'That's pretty.'

'Bit tatty since Luke put it in the washer with the footie things. Besides I'd need something to go with it. I always wear it with jeans for the school disco and this isn't a jeans type do.'

'Ask Dad for something new.'

'Did. He told me to wear the dress I wore to be bridesmaid at Auntie Brenda's wedding last year.'

Even Emma pulled a face at that suggestion. The dress was a candy pink meringue with puffball sleeves and I felt like I belonged on top of a Christmas tree when I wore it. Sexy. Not.

Emma went back into her drawer and pulled out her Barbie savings bank. She opened it up and handed me two twenty pence pieces. 'Here you can have all my money.'

I gave her a hug. 'Thanks, Em. You're a star.'

She can be so sweet when she wants to be.

I put all my clothes back, then went downstairs to watch telly with the others. I felt miserable. This was the first time I'd ever been invited to anything so glamorous. Lia's sister Star was coming down from London with all her model friends, half the rock music industry was going to be there, then there was Mrs Axford who always looked like she stepped out of *Vogue* and, of course, Ollie. And Jade. No doubt she'd have some fabulous little number planned and I, I was going to look like the back end of a bus. I'm sure Mum would have understood if she'd been here. Dads don't understand the importance of looking your best on occasions like this, not my dad, anyway.

'Why do you want money to buy an outfit you'll only wear once and put back in the cupboard?' he'd said.

It wasn't fair.

It was all right for Lia and Becca. They had mums to take them shopping. Lia had been up to London with hers and come back laden with designer carrier bags full of gorgeous things wrapped in tissue. Her mum had got her the works: mucho sexy high heels, a diamante choker that looked like it cost a bomb and a powder blue lace mini-dress. She'd even got new sexy underwear and make-up. She looked a million dollars when she tried it all on.

Becca's mum had also let her have something new. She'd taken her up to Exeter and Becca had chosen a black sleeve-less top with a feather trim, tight black satin trousers and really high black mules. She looked eighteen and really sophisticated.

I could just see me turning up in my candy pink brides-maid dress. I'd be the laughing stock. There's no point, I thought, as I tried to concentrate on the telly. I'm not going to be able to go.

Dad must have been feeling guilty, because he kept glancing over at me. 'Cheer up, love.'

'Uh,' I said.

'Honestly, Cat, with your looks, you'll be the belle of the ball. You don't need fancy clothes to stand out in a crowd.'

'Yeah right.' I said. You really *really* don't understand, I thought.

Just at that moment I spotted something on the bookshelf behind the telly. Stacked in with the photo albums and gardening books. That's *it*, I thought. My fairy godmother. Of sorts.

I waited until Luke, Joe and Emma had gone to bed and Dad had gone to make a cup of tea, then pulled the catalogue off the shelf, ran upstairs and locked myself in the bathroom.

I flicked through the pages until I found the teen evening wear section. A treasure trove of seriously cool clothes, sequinned tops, beaded dresses, silky fabrics, velvet trousers. Fab, *fabtastic.*

I checked the terms.

You pick what you want.

You phone up.

They deliver within forty-eight hours.

You return the item if it's not right.

It would be *so* easy. The party was in four days. I just had time. And after the party I could return the item as 'unsuitable'. No harm done. Dad need never know. He'd bought a lawnmower from them in the summer and a statement with his account number was in the front of the catalogue. *So* easy.

I flicked back through the pages. There was so much to choose from. Gorgeous colours, glittery, glamorous, girlie. I wished Lia or Becca were here to help me, but I decided there and then not to tell them. On one page there was a one-shouldered dress in purple silk. The business. That would do it.

Then a thought struck me. Was it bad? It wasn't *really* stealing as I'd return the dress the morning after the party. But a shadow of doubt crept in after all my efforts to be truthful. *Would* it be wrong? Dishonest? Dad need never see it, so I wouldn't have to lie about it and I'm sure that Lia and Becca would understand. I would just be borrowing the dress. Surely that was OK?

The dress was staring back at me from the glossy page. It would look *soooo* good. I could just see myself in it. No harm done, I told myself, no harm done. And I'm sure my mum would have let me have it if she'd been here.

I unlocked the bathroom door, crept down the stairs, picked up the portable phone then crept back up again.

I dialled the number before I could change my mind.

Party On

'YOU LOOK top,' said Lia, when I came out of her bathroom.

I went to look at my reflection in her wardrobe mirror. The dress looked great.

'Not sure about the sandals though,' I said. I hadn't dared to order shoes from the catalogue as well, so I had to wear my strappy black ones from the summer. They didn't go with the dress and looked a bit cheap next to Lia's and Becca's sexy mules.

'You could go barefoot,' suggested Becca, 'like that singer from the sixties.'

'Sandie Shaw,' said Lia. 'I think Dad sent her an invite, but I don't know if she's coming.'

'Barefoot at five foot two,' I laughed. 'I don't think so, people will think I'm about nine years old.'

Lia's bedroom door opened and in walked one of the most beautiful girls I'd ever seen. Like Lia, she was blond and willowy, but her hair was cut spiky short showing off her cut-glass cheekbones perfectly.

'You must be Cat and Becca,' she smiled at us. 'Lia's told me all about you.'

'And you must be Star,' I said. 'Do people say that they're star-struck when they meet you?'

'Yeah,' she laughed as she took in our outfits. 'Particularly naff men who think that they're the first one to come up with it. So. *Look* at you three. Watch out boys, three stunning girls to choose from – a blond, a brunette and a redhead. ' Then she saw my feet and sighed. 'What size shoe are you, Cat?'

'Thirty-six.'

'Ah. Perfect,' she said and disappeared only to reappear a minute later with a shoebox. 'Here, try these,' she said getting out the most divine pair of shoes. 'Rule one of any outfit, make sure your shoes don't let you down.'

She handed me a pair of purple suede shoes with a kitten heel and a little suede flower on the toe.

'They're from Emma Hope,' she said as I nodded like I knew who Emma Hope was. 'Sexy, but unlike some high heels, you can actually walk in them.'

'So what's rule two of any outfit? I asked as I tried the shoes on.

'Make sure your underwear doesn't let you down,' she replied.

'I thought that was for when you had an accident,' said Becca. 'My gran was forever saying that when we were little. Make sure your underwear's clean in case you get run over.'

'Not what I was thinking of,' laughed Star, then winked at me like I knew what she meant.

The shoes looked gorgeous. The exact shade of my dress and suddenly the whole outfit came together.

'You shall go the ball,' said Becca.

'Story of my life,' I explained to Star.

After Becca had done her usual 'does my bum look big in this?' routine and we'd assured her that it didn't, we applied few squirts of perfume, a slick of lip gloss and we were ready to make our entrance.

The party was in full swing when we got downstairs. My stomach felt all fluttery with excitement as we took in the atmosphere – people chatting and laughing, the clink of glasses and sound of champagne corks being popped. Mrs Axford had lit the house with candles and it looked wonderfully romantic bathed in the soft honey light.

'What's that divine smell?' I asked Lia.

'Jasmine. Mum bought scented candles. It's heavenly isn't it?'

I nodded. Heavenly was the word. Everyone looked *sooo* glamorous in little cocktail dresses and gorgeous shoes. I was glad I'd bought my dress as, looking at all these guests, I'd have been way out of place if I hadn't made an effort. I could see Squidge, busy going from room to room videoing, and he gave us a little wave when he saw us, then pointed the camera at us for a few seconds before moving off again. He looked like he was in his element.

'I'm just going to check on a few people,' said Lia. 'Back in a mo, so help yourselves to drinks and whatever.'

Becca and I both felt shy and star-struck at all the famous faces in the crowd. We stood near the banisters, at first, doing our best not to look too gobsmacked as stars we'd only ever seen on MTV walked past. And here they were in the flesh. At the *same* party as us.

'Oh my God,' said Becca. 'Isn't that the guy from that band, The Heartbeats?'

I turned to look. 'Yes, it is. Oh Bec, I don't think I'm going to have the nerve to get up and sing in front of this lot.'

'Rubbish,' said Becca. 'It's only one number and we couldn't have practised it more. By the way, have you seen Jade yet? She was bringing the backing track.'

A few moments later I saw Jade coming towards us through the crowd. She looked fabulous as well, in a short white leather mini and studded jacket.

'Very rock chick,' I said.

She was in a good mood. 'Thanks. And I like your dress. Actually, I was looking for you. We're on soon in the green room.'

'Have you got the tape?' I asked.

'No,' she said. 'You were bringing it.'

'No I wasn't,' I said. 'I gave it to you.'

'You did not.'

'Did.'

I wasn't going to ruin the evening by arguing. 'Look. It's a popular song so we need to find Lia and ask if, by any miracle, she's got a CD with the track on it, so at least we can sing along.'

'Good plan,' said Becca, who was looking daggers at Jade.

'You go that way Bec,' I said pointing right. 'Jade, look upstairs and I'll go that way. Meet you back here in ten minutes. Then perhaps we could have a run through in Lia's bedroom.'

I felt a bit shy walking about on my own, but it was flattering in a way, as I was getting quite a lot of looks from the men there. So they were ancient, but it was still nice to be noticed.

'Looking good.' Mac grinned as he passed by with a tray of drinks.

'So are you,' I said. 'That waiter's outfit suits you.'

'So it does,' purred a middle-aged blond lady as she took a drink. 'I *love* a man in uniform.'

Mac went behind her and did me an 'arghhh' face.

I wandered into the green room where the talent hour had already begun. A woman who looked familiar from Cable TV was singing and playing the piano. She was brilliant and the crowd applauded like mad when she finished. I stayed to listen for a moment whilst scanning the room for Lia. Ollie was on the opposite side and, when he saw me, he put his hand on his heart then blew me a kiss. I felt really chuffed. It was going to be a great party.

Next up on stage was a woman who sang a Madonna song. She was awful, truly awful and I tried not to catch Ollie's eye because I knew I'd laugh. After she'd finished, the crowd applauded madly again and as she got down I heard people saying, 'Well done,' and, 'Brilliant show'.

We're all fibbers, I thought, and sometimes it's right to be. If anyone had said, 'God you were awful', it would have ruined her night. The guests' reaction confirmed to me yet again that there definitely was a time and place to be kind with a small lie. As Mrs Axford announced the next act, I remembered I was supposed to be looking for Lia so dragged myself away.

I looked in two of the living rooms on the left but there was no sign of her. No sign of Jade or Becca back at the banisters, so I decided to try Mr Axford's study. When I opened the door to look in, it was empty, but I paused to take in the atmosphere.

Like the rest of the house, it was bathed in candlelight and someone had lit a fire in the grate. It looked so cosy, like an old gentleman's club on a film set with its wood-panelled walls, dark leather sofas and tall bookshelves full of books. I couldn't help having a peek at some of the framed photos of Mr Axford when he was on tour with his band, Hot Snax. Suddenly two hands slipped round my waist and gently pushed me further into the room.

Ollie shut the door, took my hand and led me over to one of the sofas. 'Come and sit by the fire, Cat.'

I perched on the sofa and he sat next to me and leaned back. He looked so sexy, and sitting there in the mega-romantic atmosphere, all the feelings I'd been pushing away came flooding back.

'Alone at last,' he said, taking my hand again.

'But you're not alone,' I joked nervously. 'I'm here.'

He laughed and put his arm around me. 'I can see that. But we haven't had a chance to catch up properly for ages. Not since the beach that time.'

I slid a few spaces away from him, but he moved close up again.

'Relax,' he said, 'I'm not going to pounce.'

I smiled. God I was nervous. I felt stupid, like an immature little girl. I didn't want him to think I was inexperienced or a Miss Prim, so I didn't move away again. Anyway, it felt nice. I liked the sensation he caused whenever he was near. Calm and chaotic at the same time.

'Has anyone ever told you that you have the most gorgeous mouth?' he said staring at my lips.

I shook my head and tried to think of something witty to say back, but too late, he'd leaned in and was kissing me.

At first I was going to push him away, but it felt so

good. He was a top kisser, soft yet firm at the same time. He pushed me down further into the sofa at the exact moment that the door opened.

'Oh, er . . . sorry. *Oh!* It's you!' said a white-faced Becca when she saw us. Then she ran out leaving the door open.

'Oh sugar, got to go,' I said to Ollie, who looked taken aback as I shoved him off and ran after Bec.

Frantically I searched everywhere for her, but she seemed to have disappeared into thin air.

'Have you seen Becca?' I asked Lia, who was chatting to Mac as he refilled his tray in the kitchen.

'I saw her heading upstairs,' said Squidge, who I suddenly noticed lying under the table.

'What are you doing down there?' I asked.

'Mrs Axford asked me to film all angles of the party,' he replied. 'The good, the bad and the ugly.'

'Hmmm,' I said as I headed for the door, 'talking of bad, you haven't seen Jade have you?'

'Saw her go into the study,' said Mac.

I couldn't resist. I had to see if Ollie was still in there and if Jade was doing her 'I'm anybody's but especially yours' routine.

I crept down the corridor, opened the door a fraction and peeked in. My heart stopped. Ollie *was* still in there. And he was snogging Jade. I felt like someone had hit me in the stomach and I reeled back in shock. Oh *God*, this is how Becca must have felt. And all over a stupid boy who doesn't care who he snogs as long as he *gets* snogged. Sugar! He was a quick worker. *How* could I have been so naive to think that I was special. Lia had warned me. She'd told me what he was like. About all those silly girls who thought that they'd be the one to make the difference.

I ran back to the kitchen and found Squidge who was now perched on top of the fridge filming down.

'Has that camera got instant replay on it?' I asked.

He nodded.

'Can you film something, or rather someone, for a mo? But don't let them see you.'

Squidge nodded again and jumped down. 'I like a bit of secret filming, makes the result more interesting. Lead the way.'

We tiptoed back down the corridor to the study and again, I opened the door a fraction so Squidge could get his camera round.

'Ah, see what you mean,' he said as he saw that they were still going at it on the sofa. He filmed for a few moments then drew the camera out.

'Please will you show that to Becca? I want to prove to her that Ollie is after anyone and it's not worth being in love with him.'

Squidge looked at me closely. 'OK. But are *you* OK, Cat? You look kind of upset.'

'I'm fine,' I said remembering something I'd heard a girl in Year Eleven at school say once. 'Fine,' she'd said. 'F.

Foolish. I. Insecure. N. Neurotic. And E. Exhausted.'

Lia beckoned to us from the stairs. 'Bec's in my bathroom,' she said. 'Do you want to go up?'

I turned back to Squidge. 'Let me have a word first, OK?'

'OK.' He shrugged. 'If you're sure you think this is a good idea.'

I ran up the stairs and into Lia's bedroom. I knocked on the bathroom door. 'Bec, it's me. Can I come in?'

'Go *away*,' she said.

'Please, Bec.'

'GO AWAY. I don't want to talk to you.'

'I thought you might like to know that Ollie is now snogging someone else downstairs.'

Silence.

'He's snogging Jade.'

Silence.

'Becca. I just want you to know he's not worth it. I didn't *mean* to snog him. I was looking for Lia and he pushed me into the study and kissed me, then you came in.'

Silence.

'He made the first move.'

Double silence.

'Oh please, Becca. He's not worth falling out over.'

I heard the door unlock.

'How do I know you're not making it up?'

'Wait here.'

I went out into the hall and called Squidge in.

'Play back the video, Squidge.'

Squidge did as he was told and showed the scene he'd just filmed. Becca watched then looked at me.

'Does Squidge know about what happened earlier?' she asked.

I felt my heart begin to beat madly in my chest. Oh, please don't say anything, I thought. Not now. Not like this. It wouldn't be fair to Squidge.

'She's been after Ollie for ages,' continued Becca, 'when we went to Rock and God knows how long before.'

I wanted to die.

'Jade's such a cow. She knew I fancied Ollie, but wasn't even going to give me a look in. I say good luck to them.'

Suddenly she put her arm through mine and smiled at me. 'They deserve each other.'

'Cool attitude,' said Squidge. 'Good on you Becca. You're right, if he hasn't noticed anyone as fab and fun as you, then forget him. Anyway, got to go, got people to film.' He put his camera up to his eye and filmed the bedroom for a moment. 'See you later.'

After he'd gone I glanced over at Becca. 'I *am* sorry Bec.'

Becca shrugged. 'Was he a good kisser?'

I wasn't going to lie about this, so I nodded.

Becca shrugged again. 'You win some, you lose some. I've been obsessing about him for weeks and he's hardly given me a second glance. And Lia did say he's a love rat.

Phff. I'm not going to let him ruin my night. And to be honest, I was beginning to get tired of thinking about him. Unrequited is not my scene.'

I gave her a huge hug. 'You are my bestest, bestest friend, Becca. Top, top, top. And I'm *so* sorry about snogging Ollie.'

'So am I. But you're right, it isn't worth falling out over is it? I've been miserable sitting there in that bathroom.'

I hugged her again. 'We've been friends for years, Bec, it's important not to let *anything* get in the way. Boys are going to come and go in our lives, but true friends are always there for you.'

'Yeah. And Lia told us what he was like. I guess it's not your fault he fancies you.'

'Me and Jade and half the world,' I said.

'Yeah maybe. But no way I'm singing with Jade tonight.'

'Fine by me. I was dreading it anyway. Though . . . we could do a knife throwing act instead.'

Becca smiled. 'With Jade as the target?'

'Exactly.'

Becca combed her hair which for once had stayed straight and sleek, then she turned to me. 'Let's forget him, shall we? Boys just *aren't* worth the agro.'

'I agree,' I said. 'Friends are much more valuable.' I joined her at the mirror then began to sing: '*Love hurts, love scars . . .*'

'*Love wounds and mars,*' she sang back, then we both laughed.

Lia came in to find us collapsed on the bed laughing.

'What's going on?'

'We just decided boys stink,' said Becca.

'My brother included,' said Lia.

'They break your bloomin' 'art,' I sighed in my best 'EastEnders' voice.

'Too right,' said Lia. 'So let's get down there and break a few of theirs.'

We redid our make-up and hair and set out for round two.

We headed for the kitchen which is where most of the boys seemed to be, all stuffing their faces with vol-au-vents and little canapés like they'd never eaten before.

Phew, I thought, as I watched Becca get talking to Mac, then laugh at something he said. Everything's going to be all right. It certainly couldn't get any worse than half an hour ago.

'I'm just going to get some fresh air,' I said opening the back door and stepping out on to the terrace.

Once outside I leaned against the cool wall and looked up at the stars. I felt sad. Although I'd done my 'I don't care' act, I was still smarting from finding Jade with Ollie. I'd thought that we had something special and that he felt the same way about me. Hah.

Big lesson, I thought. *Big* lesson. Not all boys are like

Squidge, dependable and faithful. If you put your trust in the wrong boy, you get hurt. I'd been so naïve.

It was then that Max and Molly noticed I was there. They must have been put out in the garden so that they didn't bother the guests. They bounded up to me with their usual enthusiasm and I tried to get away before they leapt up with muddy paws. I opened the door to get back inside, but too late: Molly caught the hem of my dress in her mouth and, as I tried to get inside, I heard an almighty rip.

Telling the Truth

'I AM *not* a liar,' I said. 'A liar is someone who tells lies. A lot. And I'm not like that. Am I? Oh, I don't know. I've tried telling the truth, the whole truth, and nothing but the truth, and that got me nowhere . . . Actually it got me detention, but you know what I mean. And now this. I feel like I'm being punished again. I can't win.'

'What are you on about Cat?' asked Mac. 'Lia told me to bring you a drink and cheer you up. What's the problem?'

I was up in Lia's bedroom wearing her dressing gown and frantically trying to mend the tear in my dress. I pointed at the rip. '*This* is the problem. No, *I'm* the problem. No. *Everything's* the problem,' I said. '*Life* is a problem, Mac. First this stupid dress. Then Squidge and Ollie and Becca and . . .'

'What about Becca?'

'She fancied Ollie, but he got off with me, then Jade. By now, he's probably been through half the girls at the party.'

'Er. Stop there a mo. *Fancied* Ollie?' asked Mac. 'Fancied as in past tense? Are you saying she doesn't any more?'

'She's seen the light, I think.'

'Really? Excellent!' Mac smiled, punching the air. 'Er, sorry, what were you saying? What's the prob?'

'*Me.* I'm the problem. I'm a liar.' I didn't care who knew any more. I was sick of living in a shadowland of my own making. I wanted to be able to talk to my friends like I used to. Tell them everything. Have a laugh. Talk about what was happening.

'You're a liar?' said Mac looking puzzled. 'About what?'

'How long have you got?'

Mac looked at his watch. 'Five minutes,' he laughed. 'I'm on my break.'

'OK. Here's the problem, or part of it. Ollie. I fancy him. I do. I know it's stupid and he's Mr Ratfink and breaks hearts all over the place, but I feel what I feel. And I know I have to get over it. But it's not that so much that's bugging me. Well it is, but it isn't.'

'So what is it?'

'I hate not being able to tell Bec everything. I'm tired of dealing with everything on my own. Bec and me, we've never had any secrets and this is the first time I've ever held back. All because of a stupid boy. Ollie. Who's down there snogging *your* stupid sister.'

'Typical Jade.' Mac grinned. 'Actually he's not any more. He's in the kitchen talking to some girl from

London and Jade's hanging about looking really miffed.'

'Serves her right,' I said. 'Now she knows how we felt. Becca got upset because he snogged me earlier. Bec's got over it because she said she doesn't do unrequited and she's sick of thinking about him. But me. Me? I'm not over it. I feel like crapola. Becca's my best mate. You confide in best mates. I want to tell her the truth.'

A cloud passed over Mac's face. 'The truth can really mess things up. Believe me, I know. You know why my mum and dad split up?'

I shook my head as I continued sewing.

'Truth. That's why they split up. Dad had an affair when we lived up in London. He told Mum the truth about it and the next thing I knew, Mum, Jade and I were packed up and moving down here. He says it was a stupid thing. One night. Meaningless, he said. He doesn't even know why he did it. He felt he had to be honest with Mum and look where it got us. She won't speak to him. So, so much for the truth. I reckon if he'd kept his mouth shut, we'd all be happy still living up in London and I wouldn't have had to leave my school and all my mates.'

'Oh, I am sorry, Mac. I never knew what happened.'

'What Mum didn't know wouldn't have hurt her.'

'Maybe,' I said. 'But something like that, it's a tough call. I mean, if I was married I think I'd want to know if my husband was cheating. Wouldn't you, if you loved someone?'

'I guess,' said Mac wearily. 'But it wasn't as though he was a serial cheater, if you know what I mean. Believe me, he really regrets it. Every time I go up there, he's always asking if she has forgiven him yet.'

'It must be really hard for you, Mac,' I said. 'Awful being in the middle.'

'He should never have told the truth,' he said bitterly.

I thought about it. I didn't want to say too much as I could tell it had taken a lot for Mac to open up and I didn't want him to think I didn't understand.

'I know you think that him telling your mum the truth ruined everything for you, but it wasn't really that, was it?' I asked.

'So what was it?'

I hesitated. 'The fact he cheated in the first place.'

'So what are you saying?'

'It was *that* that caused the trouble. Not him telling the truth. If he had been faithful, he wouldn't have had to confess.'

Mac looked thoughtful. 'Yeah. Maybe.'

'Oh I don't know, Mac. Relationships are a complicated business. Believe me, I know. You want to be truthful, but you don't want to hurt people. I don't know your mum except to look at and I don't know your dad at all. Maybe things weren't right in the first place if your dad had an affair.'

Mac nodded. 'Maybe. I don't know, Cat. All I'm saying

is that, seeing what happened with my mum and dad, you've got to be prepared. If you do decide to tell the truth, it may have repercussions.'

I looked down at my ruined dress. 'Yeah, but so does being dishonest. Like for your dad. Having to tell the truth was a repercussion of being dishonest. He obviously felt bad about it, guilty, and decided to take responsibility for his actions. At least if you tell the truth, you can sleep at night.'

Mac looked sad again. 'Yeah. But you might have to sleep in separate houses.'

The next day I decided it was time to get my life back in order. I got up, got dressed and headed straight out.

'Won't be long, Dad,' I said. 'Got a few things I have to do.'

First I went to the newsagent's and signed up to do a paper round until Christmas. So it meant getting up at six in the morning, I didn't care. I had to earn enough money to pay for the dress. Lia had offered to cover the cost, saying that it was her problem as well as mine as they were her dogs, but I refused. I wanted to take responsibility for my actions and the repercussions. All of them.

Next I cycled over to Squidge's house. On the way, I thought about Mac's mum and dad. Poor Mac. He'd lost out because of honesty *and* dishonesty. They were like two sides of a coin. But on balance I decided, I think I'd rather know the truth. Holding back on the truth is dishonest too. I'd really learned that it only prolongs the agony and I wished I'd told Squidge it was over weeks ago.

Squidge grabbed his jacket when I called for him and we headed down towards Cawsand Square.

I wasn't going to wait for the right time or the right place. If I did I'd be waiting for ever. Dive in, I told myself.

'Squidge. You know I think the world of you and I hope we can be mates for ever. I'll always be there for you when you need a friend, but the boyfriend/girlfriend thing isn't working for me any more.'

'OK,' he said.

'*OK?* Did you hear what I said?'

'Yeah. You want to finish.'

I looked at his face. He seemed OK. No shock. No tears. *Nada.*

'Well, er, how do you feel about it?'

'Cool. Good idea, I think,' he said. 'It's a fact. Life is about evolution. Things move on. Change. Evolve. I think you're right – we should move on.'

I was *gobsmacked* at his reaction. *Double* gobsmacked. 'I thought you'd be upset.'

'Not if we can stay friends, Cat. I'd be upset if you didn't want to be friends any more.'

I took his hand. 'Friends for always, Squidge.'

'Well that's OK, then.' He grinned. 'I've been thinking the same thing. See if I'm going to be a film director and write my own scripts, then I need to experience life. New challenges and that means new relationships. I think it will be good for both of us to move on.'

'How long have you been feeling like this?'

'Since summer, really.'

'Why didn't you say anything?'

Squidge shrugged. 'It's hard letting go. Didn't want to upset you. And part of me wondered if it was a mistake. I mean, you are pretty special. Maybe I'll never find anyone like you ever again.'

All the stuff I'd been thinking! 'So you've wanted to tell me for weeks?'

Squidge nodded sheepishly. 'I was going to tell you that time I gave you the bracelet. I wanted it to be a kind of memento of our relationship. But I couldn't find the right words.'

'I know what you mean,' I laughed. 'So we're OK?'

He nodded again.

'Squidge. No matter what happens. Where we end up. Who we end up with. We will always be each other's first love. No one can ever take that away.'

'Yeah,' said Squidge, then gave me a huge bear hug. 'Cat Kennedy, my childhood sweetheart. Maybe I'll write a film about you one day. Now. Let's go and get a pasty. I'm starving.'

Cat-harsis

I WOKE up the next morning feeling brilliant. Full of hope. Everything was going to be all right.

'Cat. Can you come downstairs?' called Dad.

I could tell by his tone of voice that something was wrong. I pulled on my school clothes and ran down to the kitchen. He was sitting at the table with a pile of mail.

'Can you explain this?' he asked holding up an invoice from the catalogue company.

I hung my head. My plan had been to intercept the postman and take care of the bill, so no questions asked. But after my wonderful day with Squidge yesterday, I'd slept better than I had done in weeks. And I'd overslept. Missed the post.

'Um . . .' I racked my brain as how to best put it.

'See,' continued Dad, 'it says here that a dress was sent last week. I rang to say I hadn't made an order, but they assured me that someone from this address phoned last week.

I took a deep breath. 'It was me. I'm sorry. I had nothing

to wear for the party and when I saw the catalogue, I . . .'
I decided to omit the part about the original plan to return
the dress. 'And I . . . I've got a job with Mrs Daly delivering the newspapers to pay for it.'

Dad was quiet. There are silences and silences, I
thought. And this ain't a good one.

'I can explain . . .'

'I don't want to hear explanations, Cat. Frankly, I'm
disappointed in you. I thought I'd raised my kids to be
honest.' And then he looked sad. 'Go, Cat, get to school.
I'll talk to you about it this evening.'

School passed in a blur. I felt numb all day, like I wasn't
quite there. Lessons went by, but God knows what the
teachers said. I tried to read my school books, but the
words swam before me on the pages.

'What's up, Cat?' said Becca on the bus home.

'Nothing,' I said. I didn't want to talk to anyone. Not
even to Becca. I'd let my dad down and I felt dreadful.
'Must be mi old hormones playing me up.'

'Is it because of Squidge?'

'No. I told you. That couldn't have gone better. I feel
like a huge weight has been lifted off my mind.'

'Doesn't look like it,' said Becca.

I smiled weakly. 'Just feeling a bit low.'

'Want to come back to mine? We could hang out, play
some music?'

'No thanks. Dad told me to be straight back.'

'Call you later then.'

After I'd left Becca at the bus stop, I set off to go home. Then I turned round and headed down to Cawsand Beach.

The light was fading, it was cold and beginning to rain when I got there. There wasn't a soul on the beach as I made my way over to my favourite spot and, as I sat down, the skies opened and it began to pour. Buckets. I didn't care. No one was about and I was going to have a good cry.

Once I started I couldn't stop. So much had happened since the summer. Feeling cut off from Becca. Not being able to tell her my secrets. Having nothing to wear for the party while my two best mates got fab new things. Then the dress from the catalogue being ripped. Becca finding Ollie snogging me. Ollie snogging Jade. Trying to tell the truth and getting in trouble with everyone. Trying to stay sane in an overcrowded house. *No one* appreciates me and how I try, I thought, as great gulps of pain poured out. Being poorer than all my friends. Having to share a bedroom with a mad midget. Finishing with Squidge. And he'd *agreed* it was a good idea. Maybe he knew I was bad underneath and that's why he was happy to finish. Maybe *no one* would ever want me ever again as long as I lived and I would die alone, lonely and unwanted. I didn't want to be me any more. Everyone always thought I was so strong and brave, so good at coping but I wasn't. I couldn't cope any longer. I felt pathetic. And Dad thought I was no good.

It was as if a dam had burst deep inside me and all the things I never dared to let myself think about, rose to the surface.

My thoughts turned to Mum and a memory came flooding back. It was after the funeral and the house was quiet after all the relatives and friends had packed up and returned to their homes. Dad had made us cheese on toast, then gone up to put Joe, Luke and Emma to bed. Not wanting to be on my own downstairs, I'd followed them up and gone into the bathroom. There was the bottle of Mum's perfume on the shelf by the window and I lifted the cap and squirted the scent into the room. It brought Mum's presence flooding back, but I realised the scent would fade. As Mum had.

Then I realised that in all the rushing and pandemonium of the funeral arrangements, Dad had forgotten to buy any loo paper and there wasn't any. That had been Mum's job.

It was at that moment that I realised I hadn't got a mum any more. No one to look after us. My mum had gone.

I sat on the loo and sobbed my heart out.

So much of what had been familiar disappeared with her – Sunday lunches, the fuss she made on birthdays and at Christmas, her words of encouragement on mornings of exams, the smell of cooking, Radio Four playing in the background as Mum got everyone sorted when I returned at night.

After that memory, there was no holding back.

I thought of all the people in the world who have lost someone as well and I cried for them.

I thought about all the bad news lately, fighting in distant places, and hatred, and people losing their families and homes and jobs.

This world is *soooo* horrible, I thought. There's so much *paiiiiiin*.

When I seemed to be running out of things to cry about, a voice in the back of my head said, *and* you're short. Cry about that as well, why don't you?

I *will*, I thought. Might as well while I'm at it. It's true, I *am* the smallest girl in my class. *And* I've got a spot coming on my chin. And the only boy I really *really* fancy is King of the Love Rats.

It felt right to be there, sobbing in the rain, staring out as the black waves swelled and broke angrily on the beach. I don't know how long I sat there, but it felt like I was one with the sea and the rain, one gushing torrent of salt water.

An Honest Woman

I DON'T know what the time was when I became aware of a figure to my right by the café. A man in a weatherproof with a torch.

'Cat,' he called. 'CAT.' His words were blown away by the gusting wind.

It was Dad.

As he cast his torch over the beach, the light fell on me and he came running over.

'Cat. Thank *God*. I've been looking everywhere for you.'

He picked me up in his arms and he felt so warm and safe that I started crying again.

'Dad . . .' I sobbed. 'I'm not dishonest. Honestly I'm not. I try to be good.'

'There, there,' he said as he carried me back to the car.

Once inside the car, I began to feel a bit stupid. And very wet.

'What were you thinking of going down there on your own in the dark?' asked Dad.

'Are you still mad at me?'

'No, Cat,' he said gently. 'I'm not mad at you. Worried. But not mad. I phoned everyone. Becca said she'd left you at the bus stop and you were coming home. Then I phoned Lia and she didn't know where you were. I've been out of my mind.'

'Mum used to bring us here when we were little.'

'I know,' said Dad. 'I remember.'

'How did you know I might be here?'

'Lia phoned back after I called her. She'd been talking to her brother Ollie and must have told him you were missing. He said to look down here.'

We sat in silence for a few moments, then Dad asked, 'Ready to come home now?'

I nodded. 'But can we talk first. Just for a few minutes.'

'Sure,' he said. 'Course we can.'

'I'm really sorry about the dress, Dad . . .'

'So am I. I should have known how much it meant to you to have something nice to wear. I'm sorry. I've not been much of a dad lately, have I?'

'No. *No*. You're the best dad in the world. It's just, I really need you to know that I didn't mean to be bad. I've been thinking about so much in the last few weeks. You wouldn't believe it. It's so hard. Sometimes when you're honest, it hurts people. But it doesn't work when you're not honest. Causes all sorts of trouble. And then sometimes it does work. I've been so confused.'

'What about, Cat? Are you in trouble? Is there something you want to tell me?'

'Yes. No. I mean I'm not in trouble. Except with you. I . . . I think it's really important that we talk to each other. About what's going on and stuff.'

Dad smiled sadly. 'Do you know how like your mother you are?'

I shook my head.

'You remind me of her in so many ways. Not only in looks, you have her spirit too, Cat. Big-hearted. She was always looking out for others, like you. And like you, she was always reminding me to be honest, talk stuff through as you say.' He paused a moment as though hesitant. 'Remember when she died?'

I nodded.

'Remember how she always said she wanted to know the truth? No lies? Well I'm going to tell you something I've never told anyone before. About when she died. It was the most difficult choice I ever had to make. See, I knew how ill she was. Only a matter of months. Weeks. I wanted to protect her and you from the truth . . .'

'So what did you do?'

Dad hesitated as though it was painful for him to remember. 'I agonised over it, but one day she asked me to be completely honest. She wanted to know exactly what her condition was so that she could prepare herself. I felt so helpless, frustrated, there was nothing I could do. But, in the end, I had to honour her wishes and I told her. She was so brave, Cat.'

'I know. I remember.'

'I couldn't give her false hope and I couldn't stop what was happening. At the very end, I tried to be there night and day, but one day I'd left her, not for long, just to get a few things from home. Change of clothes and that. The nurses told me afterwards that she was slipping away and they thought it was her time, but she came round for a moment. She asked the nurse where I was, the nurse explained I'd be back in about half an hour. Then she slipped back into unconsciousness. When I came back, I knew she didn't have long, they didn't think she'd regain consciousness. Then all of a sudden, she opened her eyes and turned and looked right at me. She took my hand, then she died.'

Dad brushed a tear away from his eyes and I reached over and took his hand in mine.

'It was like she'd waited for me. She wanted me there as she passed away. And Lord knows, it was important for me to be there. I realised afterwards that if I hadn't told her the truth, and she hadn't known that she was dying, then she might have slipped away when I wasn't at her bedside and I couldn't have lived with that, Cat. It meant everything that I was there, you know, by her side, holding her hand when she went.'

'I was glad I knew as well,' I said. 'It gave me time to get used to the idea. If she'd just gone one day and I hadn't understood how ill she was, it would have been even worse. She wasn't afraid of the truth, Mum. And I'm not going to be either.'

'You're right, Cat. As she was right then. And now, the most important thing is for us to keep talking about whatever. We're family and there's so much untruth in the world, we shouldn't have it at home.'

'I understand,' I said. 'That's why you were so disappointed in me.'

'Only for a moment, Cat. If you only knew how proud I am of you really.'

I felt choked. 'Thanks Dad and I'm glad you told me about Mum. You've been brave too. I'm proud of you.'

'So how about I take you home? We get you into some warm clothes, make a mug of hot chocolate and then I'll cook you one of my specials.'

I suddenly realised I was starving. 'Er, seeing as we're being honest here . . .' I smiled. 'How about we skip the home cooking and get some chips?'

'Excellent idea,' Dad said, grinning as he started up the car.

As we drove home, I felt closer to him than I ever had in my life. And we didn't stop talking. We talked about accepted lies, like telling kids that there's a Santa and a tooth fairy. Cowardly lies, compassionate lies, lies to make you buy things, political lies, false promises and we both agreed again that with us, with family, there was no room for any of them.

'In the end,' said Dad as we pulled up in our drive at the back of the house, 'honesty is best but it's important to be aware of people's feelings when you have something to say. Sometimes you have to adjust the truth. More important, though, is to be true to yourself.'

'OK,' I said turning to him before I got out the car. 'So, er, one more thing. Um . . . Jen. Don't you think it's time you made an honest woman out of her?'

Dad laughed. 'Maybe. Maybe I just will. You'd like that, would you?'

'I'd love it. So would Luke, Joe and Emma. We know that no one will ever replace Mum, but . . .' I remembered what Squidge had said to me the day before, 'life moves on. Evolves. There's good times and bad. Joy and pain. Mum's not coming back and I think she'd want you to be happy.'

'My little girl.' Dad smiled at me. 'Not so little any more, eh?'

Options are Open

IT WAS three weeks later when we got the news.

I was doing my homework up in my bedroom when Luke came in. He looked a bit worried.

'Dad wants to see us all in the kitchen now,' he said.

'Is someone in trouble?' I asked.

Luke shrugged. 'Dunno. Jen's with him. He looks pretty serious.'

Oh dear, I thought, as I followed him down the stairs. Since my epic wailing on the beach, everyone had been getting on better than ever.

When I got to the kitchen, Dad, Joe and Emma were already seated around the table. Jen was making tea.

'Want a drink before we start, Cat?' she asked.

I nodded and tried to gauge the atmosphere. Something was going on, but I couldn't tell if it was good or bad.

'Right,' said Dad as we all settled down. 'I have something I want to say to you all.'

We all looked at each other wondering who had blown it this time and why we'd all been gathered to hear about it.

'Don't look so worried. It's good news,' Dad assured us. 'At least, I think it is.' Then he smiled over at Jen. 'Two things. First, I've asked Jen to marry me and she's said yes.'

'Hurray,' shouted Joe as Jen smiled shyly.

'We'll probably have the wedding in the spring . . .'

'Fantastic,' I said, then sang, '*Congratulations* . . .'

The others joined in, '*And celebrations* . . .'

'I hope Cat and Emma will be my bridesmaids,' said Jen looking at us both.

'You bet,' said Emma, then looked worried. 'We won't have to wear pink meringues like Cat's horrible dress, will we?'

'No,' said Dad and gave me a wink. 'You can go up to London with Jen and pick out your dresses yourselves.'

'*London!*' I said. 'Fantastic. I've never been. So what's the second thing, Dad?'

'Well, it's not definite yet,' he said, 'but we were thinking of moving after the wedding. With two incomes coming in, we could maybe afford to buy something with a bit more room.'

In front of him, he had a pile of papers. 'We've been looking at a few places just to get an idea of prices.' He handed round the papers.

There were a number of properties. One showed a white

semi-detached house on the outskirts of Millbrook, near Becca's. I quickly read the details. 'Oh my God. This one's got a large garden at the back and oh, it's got *four* bedrooms, Dad. Could we really afford something like this?'

'We'll see.' He was grinning. 'We've got to do all our sums yet. But I thought it was about time you had your own room at last, Cat.'

My *own* bedroom. I couldn't believe it.

'That's not fair,' cried Luke taking the sheet of paper. 'Four bedrooms. One for you and Jen. One for Cat. One for Emma. What about *us*? I can't stand sharing with stinky feet . . .'

'Ah,' said Dad. 'We've thought of that. If, or rather, *when* we move, we thought we'd get you a tent for the garden.'

'Brilliant!' said Joe.

'But . . . but . . . it will be cold,' said Luke.

'Only joking,' beamed Dad. 'I wouldn't put you in the garden, you daft nonce. Anyway it's early days, but you never know, in a place like that, all you need is planning permission to build in the loft and we could put an extra bedroom up there.'

'Bagsy me,' said Joe.

'No me. I'm older than you. Me. Tell him, Dad,' said Luke.

Dad looked to the heavens. 'Fighting already and we've only just started talking about it. We'll sort out who has which room when we get wherever we're going to.'

'I have some news too,' announced Emma.

'And what's that?' asked Dad, turning to her.

'I've got nits!' she exclaimed proudly.

Luke and Joe scraped their chairs back and moved away from her. Jen went and had a look through Emma's hair and grimaced at Dad.

'One of the joys you're taking on, Jen,' said Dad.

Jen smiled back. 'Can't wait . . . Combing through nit-infested hair, mmm, can't wait!'

'When will we move, Dad?' I asked.

'Not sure yet, Cat. Moving house costs money, so we'll have to save up a bit. But I wanted to talk to you all about it first and if everyone's happy, we'll go ahead with working out finances in the next few months. So. Any objections?'

No one said a word.

'Excellent,' said Dad. 'In the meantime, all options are open.'

My very own bedroom. It may be months away, but already my head was full of ideas for paint and fabric. Lia and Becca could help me. I couldn't wait.

After the family conference I ran upstairs to phone Becca.

'That's fantastic,' she said. 'Oh, I hope you buy the one near me. We could walk home from the school bus together.'

'I know. Want to come round and celebrate?'

Becca went quiet, then giggled.

'What, Becca? What's going on?'

'Um. I've got a date.'

'Who with?'

'Mac.'

'Mac! When did all this happen?'

'At Lia's party, sort of. He was so kind when I was all freaked out and I realised that I really like him. He's OK when he drops the 'I don't care about anything' act and is himself. He's called a few times and he just phoned now to ask if I wanted to go and hang out this evening.'

'So Ollie's history?'

'Well he is for me, Cat.'

'What do you mean?'

Becca went quiet on the other end of the phone. 'I know I liked him, but what's true one moment can change.'

'Tell me about it! I almost blew a fuse trying to work out how I felt about him and Squidge. It changed every day, so don't get me started on all that again.'

'OK. But just one thing I have to tell you. I could tell Ollie liked you as soon as I saw you with him at Rock, the way he looked at you. I feel rotten because I was jealous and even though I said I fancied him first, I should have said something, but I was too mean. I'm sorry, I've been a crapola friend . . .'

'No you haven't. I've been a crap friend. I always fancied Ollie, but didn't want to get in your way. But I should have told you in the beginning . . .'

'Yeah, you should. But it wasn't your fault he fancied you not me, so I'm the crap friend.'

'No, I am.'

'No, *I* am,' she insisted.

'No, I am.'

'OK. We both are. Totally crapola. But best friends are for ever and as you said at Lia's, that's worth more than any stupid boy. But if you want to go out with him, I won't mind. Honest.'

'Nah . . .' I began.

'Do you *like* him?'

'Yes. But I don't know if I'd want to go out with him.'

'Well, as long as you know that whatever happens, I'm cool.'

After I'd finished talking to Becca, I called Lia and told her all the news. She was as delighted for me as Becca had been.

'And Cat, you know Ollie still keeps asking after you?'

'Does he?'

'Want me to say anything to him?'

'Nah,' I said. 'Not really.'

'Keeping your options open?' she asked.

'Exactly. I want to enjoy being free for a while. No secrets, no lies, no truths I have or haven't to tell. It's great. So much has changed since the summer, it's like a whole new chapter beginning. Dad's getting married, we may be moving. I'm not in a relationship any more. Who knows what might happen.'

'Who knows,' said Lia. 'But Ollie did ask for your e-mail address. Can I give it to him?'

'Why not?' I grinned down the phone. 'Options are open.'

I flopped on the beanbag next to her. I felt happy. Iz and me. Me and Iz talking about stuff and Iz predicting my future.

'What does it say, Madam Rose?'

'Oh interesting,' Iz murmured. 'Very interesting. The card that crosses you is the Wheel of Fortune. It signifies a new chapter. A turning point.'

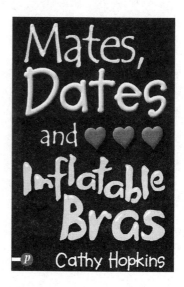

But a turning point is exactly what Lucy does NOT want. Everything is changing around her, and suddenly she is required to make all sorts of decisions.

• Everyone else knows who and what they want to be except her.
• Izzie has become friends with the glamorous Nesta and Lucy isn't certain she likes this new threesome.
• Nesta and Izzie look sixteen, but Lucy, at fourteen, can easily pass for a twelve-year-old.

But then the day Lucy sees the most wonderful boy crossing the street, things do start to change – in all areas of her life . . .

If you would like more information about
books available from Piccadilly Press and how
to order them, please contact us at:

Piccadilly Press Ltd.
5 Castle Road
London
NW1 8PR

Tel: 020 7267 4492
Fax: 020 7267 4493

Feel free to visit our website at
www.piccadillypress.co.uk